URBAN OUTLAWS

BLACKOUT

PETER JAY BLACK

BLOOMSBURY

LONDON   NEW DELHI   NEW YORK   SYDNEY

Bloomsbury Publishing, London, New Delhi, New York and Sydney

First published in Great Britain in February 2015 by Bloomsbury Publishing Plc
50 Bedford Square, London WC1B 3DP

www.bloomsbury.com

Bloomsbury is a registered trademark of Bloomsbury Publishing Plc

A CIP catalogue record for this book is available from the British Library

ISBN 978 1 4088 5145 6

Typeset by Hewer Text UK Ltd, Edinburgh
Printed and bound in Great Britain by CPI Group (UK) Ltd, Croydon CR0 4YY

1 3 5 7 9 10 8 6 4 2

Dedicated to my mother

CHAPTER ONE

JACK FENTON SAT ON THE PAVEMENT NEXT TO Charlie. He shivered and pulled a dirty blanket up to his neck.

They were opposite an apartment block near Hyde Park, London. On the ground floor, through a set of glass doors, they could make out a concierge sitting behind a desk, reading a magazine.

There was a clock on the wall above his head and its second hand seemed to be moving way too fast.

'They're an hour late,' Jack whispered into the microphone on his headset. 'If they're any later, we'll have to –'

'Relax,' a voice said in his ear. 'It'll be fine.' Obi was back at their headquarters, surrounded by sophisticated computers that could tap into CCTV systems around London.

'What if they don't deliver it?'

'They will.'

Jack sighed. This was a special mission they were doing for Obi and they couldn't let him down. Obi used to live in the apartment building, so he was the right person to guide them through the next half an hour or so, but Jack felt uneasy about it. He was used to being in control. 'What if they deliver it to the wrong place?' he said.

'They won't.'

'How do you know?' Jack glanced at Charlie. 'Wait, you do realise we have no way to –'

Charlie's bright green eyes widened and she pointed at a delivery van as it turned into the road.

Jack let out a breath. 'Thank God.'

'Told you so,' Obi said. 'Get ready.'

The van stopped in front of the apartment block's entrance and the driver hopped out. He walked to the back of the van, whistling as he went, and threw open the doors.

Charlie unzipped her backpack and took out a device shaped like a satellite dish, only this was a lot smaller. It was one of her homemade gadgets – a directional microphone, able to pick up the faintest whisper from a hundred metres away. She connected it to her headset so they could all hear.

Jack pressed a pair of mini binoculars to his eyes.

With a lot of grunts and moans, the delivery guy loaded a box on to a set of sack trucks and wheeled it to the glass doors.

He pressed the buzzer.

The concierge lowered his magazine.

The delivery driver nodded at the box.

After a few more seconds' hesitation, the concierge typed a code into a keypad on his desk.

Jack closed his eyes and listened to the tones the keypad made in his headset. When he opened them again, the delivery driver was wheeling the box across the foyer.

'Did you get it?' Obi said.

'Yeah,' Jack whispered, keeping his attention on the building opposite.

The concierge stepped around the desk, scratching his head.

Charlie adjusted the directional microphone and his voice came through their earpieces.

'Bit late for a delivery, isn't it?'

'Last one of the day,' the delivery driver said.

'Who's it for?' the concierge asked.

The delivery driver set the box down and checked

the details on his mobile computer. 'Paul McCart-
ney.' He held it out for the concierge to sign.

The concierge's eyebrows rose. '*The* Paul Mc-
Cartney?' he said. 'The guy from the Beatles?'

The delivery driver shrugged. 'I dunno.'

Jack looked at Charlie and rolled his eyes, while
Obi sniggered in their ears.

The concierge crossed his arms. 'There's no one
here with that name. You'll have to take it back.'

'Not likely,' the delivery driver said. 'The address
is right. See for yourself.'

The concierge didn't move.

'Look, mate. Just sign it, please? If no one claims it
in the next few days, you can call the number at the
bottom of the form and we'll pick it up again. It's Friday
night, I gotta get home to the missus. She'll throw a fit
if I'm not back before eight. Last time she –'

'All right, all right,' the concierge snapped. 'Give it
here.'

The delivery driver thrust the mobile computer at
him.

The concierge signed the screen and handed it
back.

The delivery driver winked. 'Cheers,' he said, and
marched to the door.

The concierge walked behind the desk and entered the security code into the keypad. To Jack's ears, it sounded like musical notes. The door lock clicked open and the delivery driver left the building.

Jack watched him drive off, then he refocused on the concierge – he was back to reading his magazine.

So far, so good.

'OK,' Obi said. 'It's time.'

There was a scratching sound.

The concierge glanced up for a moment, then continued reading.

There was another scratching sound.

The concierge put his magazine down and listened.

There it was again.

He stood up and walked around his desk, following the sound, turning his head left and right, trying to locate where the noise was coming from. He paused for a moment, then bent down with his ear to the box.

The scratching sound was coming from inside.

The concierge continued to listen, unaware a tube had now slid out of a hole in the side of the box and was pointed directly at him.

A small blast of gas hit him square in the face and he straightened up with a look of surprise. He staggered sideways and gripped the edge of the desk for support. He swayed there for a moment, then stepped behind it and picked up the phone's receiver.

He began to dial.

Jack's stomach tightened. 'No, no, no.'

But the concierge stopped dialling and his eyes lost their focus. He rocked backwards and collapsed in the chair. The phone slipped from his fingers and clattered to the floor.

The concierge gave a final jerk and fell unconscious.

Jack stared at Charlie. 'What was that gas stuff?'

She grinned. 'Best you don't know.'

'We'll have to use that again sometime.' Jack focused the binoculars at the box as the tip of a penknife blade poked out and, from the inside, someone cut open the tape securing the flaps.

The blade retracted and, after a few seconds, a head with blonde flowing curls popped out and looked around.

Wren was only ten – five years younger than Jack and Charlie – and the smallest of the Urban Outlaws.

Hence she'd been the ideal one to use for this part of the mission.

'Let's go,' Jack said, getting to his feet.

Charlie stood and slid the directional microphone back into her hard-shell backpack.

Jack adjusted the camera on his shoulder. 'Image good?' he asked Obi.

'Yep. I can see everything.'

Jack glanced up and down the road. 'CCTV?'

'No one's watching.'

Jack and Charlie hurried to the front door of the apartment building.

Wren smiled and waved at them.

Charlie waved back.

'Get a move on, guys,' Obi said. 'Someone might come.'

Wren climbed out of the box and walked behind the desk.

Jack closed his eyes and remembered the precise sounds the keypad had made. 'The code is: two, seven, seven, eight . . . three, five, five.'

Wren typed in the numbers, the door buzzed and the lock disengaged.

Jack pushed it open and gestured Charlie through.

'That was clever,' she said.

'I know.'

Charlie cocked an eyebrow at him. 'Captain Modest.'

They smiled at each other as they marched across the foyer.

'Good job,' Charlie whispered to Wren.

Wren rubbed her neck. 'I thought I was never gonna get out.'

Charlie ruffled her hair. 'You were brilliant.' She turned away and whispered into her mic, 'Obi, you said the lift's down this hallway, right?'

'Yep.'

Charlie looked at Jack. 'See you there.'

He nodded.

Charlie and Wren jogged around the corner and disappeared from view.

Jack opened the door behind the desk, grabbed the back of the chair and wheeled the unconscious man through.

The room beyond was a few metres square. Against the back wall was a small table with a kettle. To the left was a door with a *WC* sign.

Jack tipped the concierge's head back and checked his breathing. Fortunately, it was steady and strong.

Satisfied he'd be OK, Jack slipped back through the door and closed it behind him. He peered around the foyer – no one was there – so he hurried down the hallway and into the lift with Charlie and Wren.

Charlie had the button panel open, exposing a mess of wires and circuitry. She had clipped a small black box with a digital readout to several of the wires behind the panel and numbers scrolled down the screen. Now and again Charlie would press a button on the device.

She glanced at Jack. 'This is taking longer than I thought.'

The lift was locked with a keypad. If they wanted to go to a specific floor, they had to hit that floor number and type in the corresponding code.

They didn't know the code to the penthouse, which Obi said was changed weekly. Charlie's code extractor would find it for them. The only problem was, it was random. She had no control over the order in which codes for each floor would come up.

'What ones have you got so far?' Jack asked her.

'Seven, one, two, six and nine.' Charlie took a breath. 'None of them close to the top floor.'

Jack's stomach tightened. Without the code, they wouldn't be going any further.

'Why can't we go up the stairs?' Wren said.

'The cameras in the stairwell are on an isolated security system,' Obi said. 'They're connected to a computer on the ninth floor.'

'We couldn't have turned them off at the concierge's desk?'

'No. He only monitors the cameras. He has no control over the main system.'

Jack and Obi had spent a long time trying to work out how to get past the cameras. There was just no way to reach the computer on the ninth floor and shut down the security system. The only other way to turn off the cameras was to use the override panels in each of the apartments. But breaking into one of them was too risky – they had no way of knowing if people were home or not.

If Jack, Charlie and Wren went up the stairs, the software would detect movement and call the security company. They would then phone the concierge, and if he didn't answer, the cops would be there in minutes.

Jack couldn't help but be impressed with the building's internal security and had to admit that he liked the challenge it posed. It was almost as if it was daring them to defeat it.

'Come on,' Charlie said through tight lips. The code extractor in her hand beeped and a series of six numbers appeared on the glowing display. Charlie hit a button to save it.

Jack looked at her. 'Penthouse?'

She shook her head. 'That was the code for the third floor.'

Jack had a funny feeling the Penthouse would be the last number the device cracked, but after another minute, it beeped again.

'Got it.' Charlie reached around the panel and hit the button to the top floor.

The doors closed and the lift started its ascent.

Jack ran through the plan. They had to get to the penthouse, bypass the alarm system and find the –

Suddenly, the lights went out and the lift came to a jarring halt.

Wren gasped.

Jack unclipped a torch from his belt and flicked it on.

'What's happened?' Obi asked.

'We're in trouble,' Charlie said. 'The lift's lost power.'

'It's not just the lift,' Obi said. 'There's random blackouts all over London.'

Charlie looked at Jack, her eyes wide. 'The virus?'

He nodded and a feeling of dread washed over him.

The virus was a sophisticated piece of software with the potential to cripple any computer. It was their fault it had escaped to the internet, and now it was taking down power stations around London. If they didn't get to it soon – Jack shuddered at the thought of how much damage the virus could do.

They had to get this mission over with as quickly as possible, get back to the bunker and work out a way to stop the virus. But first . . .

He shone his torch at the ceiling.

For a few seconds, Jack imagined crawling on to the roof of the lift.

The building was twelve storeys high and they had no climbing gear. Besides, as far as Jack knew, the shaft didn't have a ladder, and even if it did, that was one risky climb.

His stomach knotted. He hated heights.

'We're between floors,' Charlie said, reading his mind.

Jack let out a slow breath and shone the torch back up at the ceiling again.

Nothing else for it.

There were nine panels and the middle one had a latch. He looked at Wren. 'Think you could unlock that for us?'

She looked up. 'Yeah.' She seemed relieved at the prospect of getting out of the confined space, even if it was going to be dangerous.

Jack cupped his hands into a stirrup for Wren to put her foot in and he lifted her up. 'Mind the shoulder cam.' He grabbed her legs, keeping Wren steady while she fumbled for the latch.

After a moment, there was a click and the centre panel swung down. Jack lifted Wren higher. She grabbed the edge of the hatch and crawled on to the roof of the lift.

Charlie was next through the hatch and once her feet had disappeared, Jack climbed up on to the handrail and sprang up, his fingers gripping the frame.

Slink would've been proud of that move.

With effort, Jack managed to haul himself on to the roof of the lift with the others.

He got to his feet and shone his torch upwards. The lift shaft stretched above them, reminding him of the tunnels beneath the city. Except this went straight up.

Jack considered waiting to see if the power would come back on, but that could be minutes or hours.

The torch beam moved to a set of doors just above their heads.

Jack slipped off his backpack and pulled out a stubby metal bar. He reached up, jammed the bar into the crack and tried to lever the doors apart.

The bar slipped free and he staggered back.

He tried again, but he still couldn't get good leverage on the doors.

When Jack failed for the third time, he swore loudly and turned to Charlie. 'Any ideas?'

She looked up and, after a moment she said, 'Do you think you could give me a boost to that?' She pointed at a flat box on the wall halfway up the fourth-floor doors.

'I think so,' Jack said. 'What is it?'

'It's the control mechanism. When the lift reaches that level, both sets of doors open. It's directly connected to the door motors and I think I might be able to do something with it.' She glanced at him. 'With a bit of luck.'

'You know what you're doing though, right?'

Charlie shrugged. 'Not so much.'

'Brilliant.'

'Of course I do, idiot.' Charlie smiled, slipped off her backpack, took out the code extractor and opened the back of it. She removed the battery and tore out a couple of wires. She placed them between her teeth and nodded at Jack.

Jack leant against the wall of the lift shaft and made a stirrup again with his hands.

Charlie put her foot in and he lifted her up.

'Guys?' Obi said in their ears. 'What's happening?'

'Trying to solve a problem,' Jack said, doing his best to hold Charlie steady.

She pulled a screwdriver from her hip bag, undid the cover to the door controls and looked inside. After a moment, she reached in and connected the battery. There was a small spark and the doors to the lift shaft opened a few millimetres. She did it again and they opened another five millimetres or so.

'All right,' Charlie whispered. 'That's the best I can do without mains power.'

Jack lowered her back down. He reached up again and jammed the bar into the gap in the doors. This time he got a better grip – he managed, with effort, to open them wide enough to get through.

Jack clawed at the bottom edge of the door

and hauled himself up. He shone his torch left and right, checking no one was around, then hoisted himself over the lip and slid on his belly into the corridor.

Next, Jack spun around and held out his hands. Charlie lifted Wren up to him and he pulled her through.

Wren leapt to her feet and pressed her back against the wall, her eyes scanning left and right, straining into the darkness as she kept a lookout.

Jack turned back to help Charlie, but she was already sliding out next to him.

She stood up and dusted herself off. 'Stairs?'

Jack shone his torch to the left. 'This way,' he whispered.

They silently crept along the corridor, listening for even the faintest sound.

At the end of the hallway, Jack opened the door to the stairwell. 'We need to move fast,' he whispered.

If the cameras came back on, they'd be in trouble.

How long would it take for the security computer to boot back up?

Jack ushered Charlie and Wren through and the

three of them raced up the stairs as fast as they could, only stopping when they reached the door to the penthouse.

Catching his breath, Jack wondered how much time they had to make up. Speaking of which – 'Obi,' he said into his microphone. 'How long do we have before the night shift starts and the next concierge gets here?'

'Fifteen minutes.'

'*What*?' Jack looked at Charlie. 'We don't have enough time.'

'Yes, we do.' It took Charlie under a minute to pick the lock and open the door. 'See?'

'Wait,' Wren whispered. 'How do we know the apartment's empty?'

'He's out for the evening,' Obi said in their ears. 'The Royal Opera House. Won't be back for another couple of hours at least.'

Jack peered in to the penthouse hallway. With the power off, at least they didn't have to bother about the alarm.

The three of them hurried inside.

Charlie stopped at the security box on the wall and cut the main wires. 'Just in case the power comes back,' she whispered.

Jack nodded and followed Wren through a set of doors.

The lounge was minimalist with stark white walls and two black leather sofas facing each other. Apart from that, there was no other furniture. Not even a TV.

'What happened?' Obi said.

'What do you mean?' Jack said, adjusting his shoulder cam and shining his torch around the room.

'What's my uncle done to this place? It used to be really homely. Where's the grandfather clock?'

Obi's mum and dad used to own the penthouse – along with a mansion or two – and, when his parents died, Obi's uncle had made off with everything. Obi and his sister didn't get a penny and that was something the Outlaws were going to change with this mission.

'Which way is it?' Jack asked.

'The door to the right,' Obi said.

Charlie joined them as they marched across the lounge and through the door.

They were now standing in a room filled with books. It seemed every available shelf was crammed full and the floor was covered with stacks of volumes. In the middle of the chaos was a leather, high-backed Oxford chair. A small side table was next to it with a multicoloured glass lamp.

The contrast to the rest of the neat, minimalist apartment was striking.

'That's more like it,' Obi said. 'He obviously hasn't touched this room. Looks exactly the same as it always did.'

'Doesn't seem as though he ever comes in here.' Jack's eyes flitted around the shelves, looking for cameras, then he aimed the beam of his torch at the far end of the room. On the wall, under a brass picture light, hung a dark oil painting. It was a portrait of a man in an old military uniform. Jack paused for a moment, soaking up every brushstroke. He adjusted his shoulder cam. 'Are you seeing this? Who is it?'

'That's my great-great grandad,' Obi said. 'He was a captain in the navy.'

Jack took a few steps forward and his headset crackled. 'Obi?' He stepped back to the door. 'Obi?'

There was no answer.

Jack looked at Charlie.

'Obi,' she said into her own headset, 'can you hear us?'

Still no answer.

'It must have something to do with the blackouts,' Charlie said.

Wasting no more time, Jack, Charlie and Wren picked their way between stacks of books and stood in front of the painting.

Charlie pressed a button on the side of the frame and swung it away from the wall. Buried in the plaster behind was a large safe, its electronic keypad lit up in green.

'How's that got power?' Jack said.

'It can run on its own backup battery for months.' Charlie slipped a screwdriver from her pocket and undid the keypad panel.

The safe would lock itself down permanently if they messed the next part up.

Charlie looked at Jack. 'This is going to take both of us,' she reminded him. 'Remember to keep an even pressure.'

Jack put the torch in his mouth and together they carefully lifted the panel's bottom edge away from the safe to allow Wren to peer underneath.

'Is it?' Charlie asked her.

'Oh, yes,' Wren said.

'Like we discussed?'

Wren nodded. 'Yep.'

With her free hand, Charlie reached into her hip bag and passed Wren a set of wire cutters.

Wren slid the cutters under the panel. 'Which wire did you say it was?'

'The blue one,' Charlie said.

'Oh.'

'Why?'

'They're both blue.'

'*What*?' Charlie peered behind the keypad. 'That's just brilliant.'

Making sure he didn't move the panel any further from the safe, Jack looked behind too and could see the anti-tamper contact switch. If they lifted the panel any further, the circuit would break and the safe would lock itself down. Wren was right though – both wires leading to it were blue. Charlie had thought one would be red.

Jack straightened up and looked at her. 'Ideas?'

Charlie sighed. 'Nope.'

'Awesome.' That meant there was a fifty per cent chance Wren would cut the right wire, and a fifty per cent chance she'd cut the wrong one. He looked at her. 'You pick.'

Wren looked shocked. 'Serious?'

'We've come this far.' Jack scanned the room again, looking for any hidden security he hadn't spotted. Still not seeing any, he turned back to Wren and nodded. 'Do it.'

Wren swallowed and reached behind the keypad. 'Cutting.'

Jack closed his eyes and held his breath.

There was a snipping sound.

For a full five seconds no one moved.

'It's OK,' Wren said.

Jack opened his eyes and saw she was now smiling. He grinned back at her.

Charlie quickly lifted away the keypad panel. Next, she took out a portable soldering iron from her hip bag, flicked it on and started working on the circuit board inside.

She joined several wires, removed a few components and then soldered a microswitch.

Jack wondered how much time they had left, but Obi still wasn't responding to their calls.

Charlie finally turned off the soldering iron and checked her work. She had to get this right the first time. No room for mistakes. She looked at Jack. 'Do *you* want to do it?'

'No thanks,' Jack said. 'It's all yours.'

Charlie took a breath and hit the microswitch.

The safe's lock clicked.

All three of them let out an anxious breath.

'Nice one.' Jack opened the safe, shone the torch inside and stared for a moment.

'What's wrong?' Charlie said.

Jack stepped aside. 'See for yourself.'

Charlie's eyes widened as she looked into the safe. 'I don't believe it.'

'What?' Wren stood on tiptoe. 'Wait, where is it?'

The safe was empty.

'Let's get out of here,' Jack muttered.

They hurried from the reading room and back into the lounge just as the lights flickered on in the buildings outside.

The three of them froze.

'That's all we need,' Jack said.

'Guys,' came Obi's urgent hiss in their ears. 'Can you hear me?'

'Yes,' Jack said.

'I've been trying to get hold of you.'

'Power cuts.'

'I know,' Obi said. 'I've had to reroute the signal through another mast. Anyway, never mind that, the night concierge has just turned up for his shift.'

Jack looked at the clock on the wall – thanks to all the delays they were seriously behind schedule. They should've been long gone by now.

They ran back down the hallway and Charlie went to step into the stairwell, but Jack held her back. 'No,' he said. 'The cameras will be on too.'

'What are we going to do then?'

Jack turned from her. 'Obi, what's happening?'

'The night concierge is looking for the other one. He's going into the back room.'

Jack grabbed the door handle and waited.

A few seconds later, Obi said, 'He's found him. Looks like he's calling the police.'

There was nothing else for it. Jack glanced at Charlie and Wren. 'Ready to run?'

They both nodded.

'Hoods,' he said.

The three of them pulled up their hoods and adjusted the bandanas over their noses and mouths, hiding their faces from the cameras.

Jack opened the door and ushered them out. As soon as the three of them stepped into the stairwell, the alarm sounded.

Jack cupped a hand over his ear, trying to block

the noise. 'Obi?' he shouted. 'Can we get out on the ground floor?'

'No,' Obi said. 'No way for you to slip past unseen.'

Charlie looked at Jack. 'Plan B?'

'Great,' Jack said with a feeling of dread. 'This just keeps getting better.' He pressed a finger to his ear again. 'Slink, we can't make it back to the ground floor. Exit's blocked.' He looked up the stairs. 'Meet us up there as quick as you can.' Jack motioned for Charlie and Wren to hurry up.

He always hated Plan B.

CHAPTER TWO

JACK, CHARLIE AND WREN BURST THROUGH THE
door and on to the roof of the building. The cold air
stung Jack's eyes as they ran to the north-east
corner.

In the distance, he could hear the unmistakable
sound of police sirens, and he gauged they'd be
there in the next few minutes.

Jack squinted at the opposite rooftop. 'Where is
he?'

Suddenly, loud music blasted Jack's eardrums. It
was a particularly nasty dubstep track – one that
seemed to have extra screeching and grinding
sounds.

A silhouette appeared on the other building and
the figure leapt over a low wall, did a forward roll
and jumped to his feet.

Jack pressed a finger to his ear. 'Slink?'

The music stopped.

'Who else would it be?'

Jack glanced at Charlie. 'Shoot the sarcastic idiot, would ya?'

'My pleasure.' Charlie unclipped a custom-built bow from her backpack, unfolded it and took aim at Slink. For a few seconds nothing moved, then she unleashed an arrow.

It flew in an arc and shot past Slink's head, missing him by a few centimetres.

He scooped up the arrow and untied the fishing line. Attached to the line was fifteen metres of string, then rope and finally steel cable.

Slink hauled it over, fixed the cable to an anchor point on his building and Charlie did the same on theirs. Slink then used a ratchet to pull the cable taut, giving Jack, Charlie and Wren a zip line to escape on.

Jack's chest tightened with anxiety. Now he was there, he wasn't sure he could actually use it.

'Me first,' Wren said, practically bouncing with excitement.

Charlie folded the bow up and handed Wren something that looked like a stubby pair of bicycle handlebars, only in the middle was a wheel and a clamp.

She hooked the handlebars to the cable, tightened the clamp and nodded at Wren.

Wren slid her hands through the loops, securing her wrists.

'Shouldn't we have harnesses or something?' Jack said, glancing over the edge of the building to the street below.

'Where's the fun in that?' Slink said. 'Harnesses are for weak people with no sense of adventure.'

'No,' Jack said, straightening up and looking at him. 'Harnesses are for those of us who actually want to stay alive.'

'You're just chicken,' Slink said. 'Go for it, Wren. I'll catch you on this side.'

Wren smiled at Jack, gripped the bars and, without hesitation, launched herself off the edge of the building.

Jack's stomach lurched, but Wren let out a squeal of delight as she accelerated down the zip line, her legs kicking the air as if she were running on an invisible walkway.

Finally, she reached the other side and Slink helped her free her hands from the loops on the bars. 'Go,' he said.

Charlie used an attached cord in order to pull the

handlebars quickly back up the zip line to the start. She motioned for Jack to go next.

Jack looked at the roof-exit door. If he was on his own, could he make it down the stairs, somehow get past the front desk and escape before the police arrived?

As if in answer, the police sirens stopped and he heard the screech of tyres.

Car doors slammed.

Slink peered down. 'The cops are going into your building.' He looked up. 'I think you should hurry.'

Jack didn't move. How long before the police realised they were on the roof?

Charlie grabbed his arm and shook him. 'Jack.'

He looked at her for a moment, then at Slink and Wren on the opposite rooftop.

'Running out of time,' Obi said. 'The cops are on their way up to you.'

Jack reached into his pocket and pulled out a coin. 'Heads you go first, tails I go. Agreed?' Before Charlie could answer, Jack tossed the coin into the air, caught it and showed her the result – heads. He stepped back. 'Go.'

Charlie hesitated.

'No time for an argument,' Jack said.

Charlie slipped her hands through the loops, gripped the bars with both hands and threw herself off the ledge of the building.

Even though this backup plan had been his idea, Jack was regretting it.

A lot.

He considered just letting himself get caught, but that would be *very* stupid. The others would have all sorts of hassle breaking him out again. He gazed across London. Huge areas of it were completely dark.

No, Jack thought. There really wasn't a decision this time. He had to get back to the bunker and find out what was going on with these blackouts.

Charlie landed on the opposite roof and let go of the bars.

Jack adjusted his hood and bandana, making sure his face was hidden, then grabbed the string and hauled the bars back.

His stomach twisted into knots as he reached up and slipped his hands through the loops. The handle-bar grips were still warm from Wren and Charlie using them.

He swallowed and, with a surge of determination, Jack stepped on to the ledge of the building. He hesitated again and did what he knew he shouldn't have – looked down.

The road below seemed like a hundred miles away.

'Oh God.'

'You've done more dangerous things than this,' Slink said in his ear.

He was right – a while back, Jack had jumped off a building with nothing but a parachute. Only thing was, that time he hadn't had long to think about it – he'd just jumped. Plus, bullets whizzing past your head made you do crazy things.

'It's easy,' Wren said.

Yeah, right.

Suddenly, there was a shout.

Jack looked over the edge of the building. In the street below were several police cars and officers.

One policeman had his hands cupped around his mouth. He shouted, 'Don't do it. Stay right there.'

A small crowd of onlookers gathered and pointed up at Jack.

Brilliant. Now he had an audience.

The door to the roof burst open behind Jack and a couple of cops ran straight for him.

No time left.

Jack took a quick breath and, keeping his eyes locked on Slink, dropped off the ledge.

There was a collective gasp from the onlookers below.

The cold air forced Jack to squint and his stomach dropped as he accelerated down the zip line. He felt the wind pushing from the right, trying to tear him free.

Jack closed his eyes and, after what seemed like forever, he reached the other building. Slink grabbed hold of him and Jack wobbled on his feet as he unclipped the handlebars from the wire.

Taking deep breaths, Jack looked at Charlie.

'See?' she said. 'That was fun. No?'

'No.'

Slink handed her the bars and she slid them into her backpack.

Jack looked at the other roof – the cops were standing at the edge of the building, their mouths open in astonishment.

'Use the cable,' Slink jeered.

One of the police officers lifted a radio to his mouth.

Jack looked down at the street as another police car pulled to the kerb and several officers surrounded the building they were on.

'Time to go.'

They hurried to a door, opened it and went inside.

One flight of stairs down, Jack held up his hand, stopping the others.

They listened as, ten or so floors below them, a door banged open and several heavy-booted feet ran up the stairs.

Slink threw open the door behind them and they ran through.

In the hallway, Jack, Charlie, Slink and Wren stayed still and listened. They could hear shouting and the boots echoing in the stairwell.

They sounded like they were only a floor or two below them already.

Jack looked at the lift – it was in use – the numbers increasing on the display. It seemed as though the entire Metropolitan Police Force was on the hunt.

Charlie opened her bag and quickly handed them all a pair of thick-rimmed glasses.

'Obi,' Jack whispered, 'are you ready?'

'Yep.'

Everyone kept still, listening to the police running up the stairs.

They were passing their floor now.

Jack held up a hand, indicating that everyone should pull back close against the wall, but he needn't have worried – the police moved on up, not stopping to check individual floors.

Jack heard the door to the roof open and close again. He looked at the lift – it was almost at their floor. The police officers would have to get off here, because the only way to the roof was via the stairs. 'OK, Obi, *now.*'

Suddenly, all the power to the building went out.

Jack slipped on his glasses and pressed a button on the arm. A tiny display flickered to life – showing an image of the hallway ahead bathed in green.

Charlie's 'night-glasses' were an ultraportable night-vision device. Each pair had a tiny camera mounted on them that could see in very low light. Above the camera was a special infrared bulb, and in front of the right lens was a screen.

Jack turned to the others. They looked weird, almost alien, with their eyes glowing a bright green from under their hoods. 'Follow me,' he whispered.

They had to be quick. The police officers stuck in the lift were dealt with, but the ones on the roof would have torches. It wouldn't be long until they realised the Outlaws weren't up there and came to investigate the rest of the building.

Jack opened the door to the stairwell and they hurried down as quietly and quickly as they could.

Halfway to the bottom, they heard the door to the roof bang open again.

'Faster,' Jack urged the others and they increased their pace.

Instead of stopping on the ground floor, the four of them continued down the stairs to the basement. Slink threw open the door and Charlie and Wren ran through.

Jack stopped and looked up the stairwell – the cops were hurrying after them, their torch beams bouncing off the walls.

No time to waste.

Jack stepped through the door and turned back to look at the electronic lock. 'OK, Obi, re-engage the power.'

There was a pause.

Nothing happened.

'Obi?' Jack's night-glasses flickered – they only had a short battery life and probably had less than a minute left before they went dark. *'Obi?'*

'It's not working,' Obi said. 'I can't turn it back on.'

'Why not?'

'There's been another power cut. The whole area's blacked out. I've lost six CCTV cameras. I can't even see the cops any more.'

Jack turned to Charlie.

'The virus,' she whispered. 'It's getting worse.'

He nodded.

The police officers sounded close now – perhaps only a floor or two above them.

Giving up on the electronic lock, Jack turned and the four of them sprinted along a narrow corridor and through a door at the end.

They were now standing in a small room. Jack looked at the power box on the wall. It still had the modification Charlie had made to it the day before – an antenna stuck out of the top, partly hidden behind a spray can.

She hurried over to the box, opened it, disconnected the control wires and manually tried the main power switch.

No luck.

Jack's night-glasses flickered and turned off. Now he was in complete darkness. He didn't have a choice – he had to use his torch. He reached to his belt and switched it on.

They heard the door at the end of the corridor bang open. 'They must be in here somewhere,' a voice said. 'No other way out.'

Slink and Charlie slid a large tool chest aside, revealing a sewer grate underneath. Charlie knelt, swung the grate open and waved Wren over. Wren sat on the edge of the hole, then clambered down the ladder, with Charlie close behind.

Jack nodded at Slink and mouthed, 'Go.'

In a couple of seconds, Slink's head disappeared down the hole.

Jack switched off his torch. As he let his eyes adjust to the darkness, he could make out the light of the cops' torches under the door.

'Power room,' one of them said. 'I bet they're in there messing with the juice.'

Jack dropped to all fours and felt for the edge of the sewer grate. He found it, swung his legs over the hole and lowered himself down. Once inside, he reached up to the grate and dragged it back into place just as the door burst open.

Jack stood on the ladder, holding his breath.

'What's this?' a voice said. 'I told you someone's been messing with the circuit breaker. Looks like they've busted it.'

'Where are they?'

Jack remained frozen in the darkness, listening.

'We'll find them, don't you worry about that. The building's surrounded. They can't escape.'

Jack watched through the bars of the grate as the torch beams moved around the room. Then the door shut and everything went dark again.

He let out a sigh of relief and hurried down the ladder. At the bottom, he flicked on his torch and turned around.

They were standing on the side path of a main sewer tunnel.

Wren was looking down at the filthy water rushing past her feet. She wrinkled her nose and covered her mouth with her sleeve.

Charlie nudged her. 'You'll get used to the smell.'

Wren looked as if she was going to be sick. 'Doubt it.'

'Just think about it,' Slink said, shining his torch on a particularly nasty piece of who-knew-what as it drifted past, 'that came from someone's –'

'*Slink*,' Charlie snapped.

Slink laughed and skipped up the tunnel ahead, singing, 'Row, row, row your poo, gently down the stream . . .'

Charlie grumbled under her breath and marched after him, with Wren close behind.

Jack glanced back at the ladder one more time, then followed them.

• • •

An hour later, Jack, Charlie, Slink and Wren reached Badbury platform – an abandoned Underground station – just as a train went past, whipping warm air through the tunnel. Light flickered off the grubby tiles and made the old posters dance, as if they were alive.

Jack loved coming this way to the bunker. It was the point where two worlds intersected – the boring, adult world above, and their secret underground domain below.

When the train had passed and it was safe, they crossed the tracks and went through a rusty metal door.

Beyond, they strode down a service corridor. At the end was a concertina door – the entrance to the lift – and they stepped inside.

Wren hung on to Charlie's arm, while Slink pulled the door shut and hit the button on the wall. The lift let out a huge groan and started to drop.

A few minutes later, a hard thud signified the descent was over. Slink pulled back the door and they headed along another corridor. The air seemed heavier somehow, darker, like a cloak protecting them from the world above.

The beams of their torches bounced off the walls and, illuminated ahead in the gloom, was an archway. They walked through and into the next tunnel.

The walls in this corridor were of rough stone and covered in a dark green slime. Water dripped in slow rhythm and antique metal lights hung from the ceiling, creating pools of yellow on the floor.

They reached a steel door at the end that looked as though it came from a bank vault. Paint flaked off its surface and revealed dark golden rust on bare metal beneath.

Slink swung the door open and they stepped into the airlock. In the top right-hand corner was a security camera and on the wall by the door was a keypad – its numbers glowing. Jack typed in a code. The airlock door hissed open and they walked through.

The converted World War Two bunker was a huge room with brick walls and pillars.

To the right was a kitchen with a fridge-freezer, breakfast bar, cooker, dishwasher and sink.

Opposite the kitchen was the lounge, with a large TV, DVD player and games consoles. There were also two comfy sofas facing each other and several beanbags scattered around the floor. On the wall, in stencilled letters was their name: *URBAN OUTLAWS*.

Next to the lounge was the games area with a pin-ball machine, two arcade machines, a racing game, a shooting game and a dance pad – all of which had been a huge pain in the neck to get down there.

Beyond the games area was the toilet, a bath-room and a corridor that led to other rooms – the electrical room, generator room, Charlie's work-shop and each of the Outlaw's own bedrooms. There was a spare room that was full of junk.

Last, on the right-hand side of the main bunker, next to the dining room, was the 'Obi Zone'. A mass of wires, screens and computers, all of which Obi used to tap into CCTV from around the city.

Obi – a kid so round that it should've been physically impossible for him to move – sat in a modified dentist's chair, scrolling through CCTV images, most of which were blank because of the blackout.

He was munching a family size bag of crisps.

Charlie stormed over to him. Obi spotted her coming, grabbed a fistful of the crisps and rammed them into his mouth.

She snatched the bag from him. 'What about your diet?'

'He *is* on a diet,' Slink said, opening the fridge. 'Seafood.' He pulled out cans of lemonade. 'Obi eats any food he sees.'

Obi went to shout a retort, but instead sprayed out a mouthful of soggy crisps.

Wren jumped clear.

'Real classy, Obi.' Slink chucked cans of lemonade to them all.

Obi wiped his mouth and looked at Jack. 'Did you get it?'

Jack shook his head. 'The safe was empty.'

Obi's eyes widened. 'No,' he said. 'It can't have been.'

'It was,' Charlie said, resting a hand on his shoulder. 'We're sorry. We tried.'

Obi bowed his head. 'I can't believe it.' He had been expecting there to be a copy of his mum and dad's will inside the safe.

Obi's parents had owned an advertising company and had been very wealthy. A few years back, they'd been killed in an aeroplane crash. It was all over the news. Obi even had a scrapbook with newspaper clippings about it.

Obi's uncle was a solicitor and had inherited everything. According to his uncle, in their will, Obi's parents had not left a single penny to him and his sister, but Obi knew differently.

'How are you so sure there is another will?' Wren asked Obi as she took a sip of lemonade. She had not been part of the Urban Outlaws when they'd started searching for Obi's dad's real will.

Obi sighed and looked at his hands as he spoke. 'When I was, like, six or seven, I woke up one night and overheard Mum and Dad talking.' He glanced at the others, then continued, 'They were chatting to my uncle about what would happen if they died. It quickly turned into an argument when the subject of money and the will came up.' Obi swallowed and kept his eyes on his hands as he twisted his fingers together. 'Apparently, Mum and Dad decided to leave everything to me and Jess.'

'What happened next?' Wren said.

'My uncle erupted in a fit of rage and stormed out of the house.' He glanced at Wren. 'Then I went to bed.'

Jack knew that Obi now wished he'd stayed up and listened to the rest of his parents' conversation.

'What's this got to do with the will?' Wren said, frowning at him.

Obi balled his fists. 'I'm positive Dad would have made a copy of the will, even if my uncle had managed to destroy the original.'

And so that was how Obi had come to ask the other Outlaws to help him find it.

First, they had looked in Obi's uncle's office in Hammersmith. But they had no luck there.

Jack hadn't been surprised by this – from what Obi had told them, his uncle sounded like a very devious character. He wouldn't be so stupid as to have any copies of the will lying around in such an obvious place – if at all.

No, what the Outlaws had to do was to find a copy he didn't know about. One Obi's dad might have kept hidden somewhere. A backup.

The next most likely place had been the apartment in Hyde Park, but now they had found that the safe was empty there too.

Jack wondered if Obi's uncle had any idea they were hunting for the will. 'So,' he said. 'What now?'

Obi sighed. 'I don't know.'

'What about Jessica?' Charlie asked.

Jessica was Obi's sister. She was twenty-four.

Obi shook his head. 'She doesn't think there is another copy, and even if there was, she reckons our uncle would've destroyed it.'

'What does she do?' Wren said. 'You know, for a job?'

Obi bowed his head. 'Works at a fast-food restaurant.'

Charlie squeezed his hand. 'There's nothing wrong with that.'

Obi looked up at her, his jaw tight. 'She's better than that. She's clever. If it wasn't for my uncle, she'd be running Mum and Dad's company.' He looked away.

'What's he like?' Slink asked.

'Who?' Obi said, glancing at him. 'My uncle?'

Slink nodded.

Obi's eyes glazed over for a moment. Finally, he looked back at them all. 'At first, he treated us pretty well, but then it just changed. One day, he had a huge argument with my sister. She wanted to go to university to do a business and law degree. My uncle refused to pay for it, said it was a waste of money

and that she should go and get married, find someone else to sponge off.'

Slink winced. 'Not cool.'

'No,' Obi said. 'It wasn't. My sister didn't put up
with it though. She had a go at him.'

'Bet he didn't like that,' Slink said.

'He kicked her out of the house.' Obi looked down
at his hands. 'I begged him to let her back in, but he
wouldn't.'

'He's sounds horrible,' Wren said. 'I hate him.
What did *you* do?'

'It was a nightmare. My uncle used to lock me in
my room. I never went to school. The social services
eventually came to investigate and he made up a
story, said that I was violent towards him.'

Slink frowned. *'You? Violent?'*

'Exactly,' Obi said. 'I stayed at the house for
another six months before he finally managed to get
rid of me too. He told the social services he couldn't
look after me any more. He forced me to go to that
kids' home.' Obi looked at Jack and Charlie. 'I know
he faked Mum and Dad's will. I just need to prove
it.'

'Hey,' Charlie said. 'We believe you, remember?'

Obi nodded. 'Thanks.'

'Speak to Jessica again. She might have another idea where a copy might be.' Charlie offered him a reassuring smile. 'It's worth a shot.'

Obi let out a breath. 'I'll try.'

Jack walked behind Obi's chair and watched the CCTV monitors as several more went dark. 'Is it the virus?' he asked.

'Yes,' Obi said. 'No one's been able to destroy it yet.'

Jack felt responsible for what was going on because it was his idea to remove the virus from a government quantum computer in the first place. Only problem was, the virus then escaped into the internet and was now wiping out electricity supplies at all the major power stations. And, to make things even worse, it wasn't a typical virus – it didn't copy itself, it moved through systems, hunting for processing power like a vampire looking for its next victim.

Jack frowned at the screens. 'What's it doing?'

'I've had trouble keeping up with it.' Obi opened another window that showed a mass of code. 'It's damaged two power stations' computer systems in the last four hours and now it's moved on again.'

Three more screens went dark as more CCTV and traffic cameras lost power.

Jack clenched his fists.

'Got it,' Obi said. 'It's just moved into another power station.'

'Which one?'

'North Royal.' Obi brought up a screen and typed a few commands. 'It's here.'

Jack leant into the screen. He recognised the virus's unique fingerprint. Its code was built out of several different programming languages all layered and interlaced together.

Jack was glad that no one else had managed to deal with the virus yet – he didn't want the government or any criminals getting hold of it. It would be like Proteus all over again – a power that could change the world, and not for the better. What could it be used for? Infecting banks? Crippling the economy? Perhaps someone could use it to blackmail governments.

But that wasn't all that bothered him – Jack's biggest fear was that someone would use the virus to track down the location of the Urban Outlaws' bunker.

They had to destroy it. And quickly.

He stared at the virus's code. 'We need to get it before anyone else does.' Jack reached for the keyboard, but the main screen went blank.

'Oh, no.' Obi clicked a trackerball.

'What's happened?' Charlie said to him.

'The virus – it's gone again.'

Everyone stared.

'What do you mean it's gone?' Charlie said.

Jack pulled the keyboard towards him and checked. Obi was right – the virus had crippled the power station's computers, moved back to the internet and vanished.

He sighed. It was so frustrating. Every time he thought they'd caught up with it, the virus escaped again.

'Does that mean we can't do anything?' Slink said.

'Not at the moment,' Jack said. 'We'll have to wait for it to show up again.'

'Good.' Slink yawned. 'I'm knackered.'

'Me too,' Wren said.

Jack looked at the clock on the main display. It was 12.30 a.m. 'I'll write a program to look out for signs of the virus.'

If they could catch it, Jack thought, perhaps they could use it on a future mission. Its power was almost limitless.

He shook himself. His priority was capturing the virus and making sure the bunker stayed hidden.

Jack flexed his fingers and set to work.

'I'm off to bed,' Slink said. 'Come and wake me if anything changes.' He ruffled Wren's hair and disappeared down the corridor.

'I need some sleep too,' Wren said, and she left.

'I've got something I need to do.' Without explanation, Charlie hurried after Wren.

Now it was Jack who was yawning. He felt exhausted, but he had to complete the program. With a determined effort, he set to work and twenty minutes later, he'd finished. He rechecked the code, then slid the keyboard back to Obi. 'That should do it.'

'Do I need to sit here?' Obi asked.

'No. You can go to bed too. The program will let off an alarm if it detects the virus.'

Obi climbed out of his chair and walked through the door to his bedroom.

Jack strode off down the corridor, noticed a light at the end and walked towards it.

Charlie's workshop was narrow with benches down each side that held all manner of electronic equipment – soldering irons, welding machines, oscilloscopes, a desktop lathe and milling machine, various tools, everything she needed to build her gadgets.

He found Charlie at the end of the room, sat at a desk, scribbling in a notebook.

Jack leant over her shoulder. She was drawing some sort of contraption. 'Watcha doin'?'

Charlie jumped, then turned and punched him. 'You nearly gave me a heart attack.'

Jack rubbed his arm. 'Bit young for one of those, don't ya think?' He nodded at the notebook. 'Going to explain?'

Charlie stared at him as if she couldn't understand why he wasn't able to work out the drawing. 'I call it a rapid winch,' she said finally, as if this clarified the matter for him.

'A what now?'

Charlie held up the notepad. 'I needed to design this while I still have it in my head.' The drawing was some kind of motor connected to a spool of cable. 'When we had to use a zip line to get off that building, I realised there's an even better way to do it.'

'Better way to do what?' Jack said. 'Almost kill ourselves?'

'Not exactly.' Charlie laid the notepad down. 'With this, we can drop off the side of a building in a controlled way.'

'*Drop?*' Jack didn't like the sound of that.

Charlie ignored him. 'The best bit is, if we need to, the winch can haul us back up really quickly.'

Jack pursed his lips as he thought of uses for Charlie's rapid winch. They could lower themselves through a skylight, take some priceless artefact from a criminal's private collection and zoom back up before any guards spotted them.

Or was that from a film he'd once watched?

Charlie turned in her chair and pointed at a motor on one of the workbenches. 'Noble gave that to me. He said the SAS and US Navy SEALs use them for hauling equipment. It's supposed to be top secret.'

Trust Noble to have got his hands on something like that. He was one of the very few adults they trusted, and from time to time he found high-tech gadgets they could play with.

Jack looked at Charlie's drawing again. 'It's clever,' he said. 'If it works.'

Charlie looked affronted. 'It'll work.'

'Hey,' Jack held up his hands. 'You're a genius. I know that. No arguments from me.'

'Thanks.'

'How long will it take you to make it?'

Charlie looked at her drawing. 'A couple of hours, but I'm not doing it now. I need to sleep.'

'I'm going to bed too.' Jack walked to the door. 'See you in the morning.'

'It is the morning,' Charlie said, concentrating on her notepad.

She had a point.

CHAPTER THREE

THE NEXT DAY, JACK AWOKE WITH A START AND sat up in bed. He'd had one of his anxiety dreams, and it had been a bad one.

A *really* bad one.

Sweat poured from his brow and his whole body shook. He took a moment to remember what had happened.

He'd dreamt that the Outlaws' bunker was filled with smoke and he was searching the corridors, trying to find the others. As the minutes passed, the smoke grew thicker. A shadow moved up ahead and Jack tried to shout, but no words came out. He went to step forward, but he couldn't. In desperation, Jack reached for the shadow and, just as he was about to touch it, he'd gasped and woken up.

The dreams varied in their horrible content, but

were always about the same thing: the threat of losing the only family he had – the Outlaws.

Still groggy, Jack looked at his clock with the Albert Einstein face on it. It was nine. He groaned and swung his legs out of bed.

There was a knock at the door and Charlie stuck her head round. 'I thought I heard you. Do you want some breakfast? Slink's on the case – he's making pancakes.'

'Yeah, sure,' Jack said. 'Has the program found the virus?'

Charlie shook her head. 'No. Obi said there's been no sign of it.'

'Great,' Jack muttered as Charlie closed the door.

He sat on the edge of the bed and stared at the opposite wall. Where was the virus now? What was it up to?

He wondered what system it was infecting and what damage it was causing.

With effort, Jack stood up, walked to the door and followed the twists and turns of the corridor to the main bunker. When he got there, Obi was in his chair. He had a plate of pancakes on his lap and was liberally coating them in maple syrup.

Slink was busy in the kitchen, preparing more, while bopping his head to a dubstep tune that was blasting his ears.

Jack rolled his eyes. Even though Slink had earphones in, he could hear every pop, squeak and grind. He walked over to the dining table and dropped into a seat opposite Charlie and Wren.

Wren had a load of pens, felt tips, highlighters and a stack of blank postcards in front of her. She was drawing some kind of animal.

Jack cocked his head. 'Is that a cat?'

Wren glanced at him. 'A panther.' She held up the postcard.

Now it was up the right way, Jack could make out the drawing easily – it was a black panther silhouetted against London's skyline.

'That's really good.'

'Thanks.' She put the postcard down and continued with the finishing touches.

Jack looked at the other completed postcards – each one was unique, with a different animal or silhouette of a person in front of various places in London. The skies were painted in bright colours and the overall effect was fascinating.

Charlie said, 'Slink was going to help Wren with maths this morning.'

Between them, they tried to teach Wren different subjects, because she didn't go to school any more. Though, with their unusual lifestyle, that was hard to do.

'I didn't feel like doing maths today,' Wren said. 'I wanted to do this.' She held up several more postcards with colourful drawings on them. 'These are Slink's.'

Slink set down a plate of pancakes in front of Jack, pulled out his earphones and joined them at the table. He picked up one of Wren's drawings and appraised it. 'You're getting really good.'

'Thanks.' Wren looked at Jack. 'Can we go RAKing today?'

Jack shrugged and glanced over at the main computer screen – still no sign of the virus.

'After you've done these,' Slink said to her, 'I'll show you how to tag a bridge.'

'*Slink*,' Charlie moaned. 'I thought you said you weren't going to do that any more.'

In Slink's spare time, he spray-painted walls and bridges with cartoons of the Urban Outlaws. The higher the bridge, and the more dangerous the location, the more fun he thought it was.

Wren beamed at him, grabbed a blank postcard and set to work on the next masterpiece.

Jack took a bite of pancake and glanced at the monitor again.

'Do you think the virus is gone?' Charlie said. 'Maybe, someone's destroyed it.'

Jack swallowed. 'Doubt it.'

• • •

Later that morning, Jack paced back and forth in front of Obi's chair. He glanced at the time – 10.48 a.m., and still no sign of the virus.

Charlie strode into the room, smiling.

'What's up with you?' Jack said.

'I've finished the rapid winch.' She looked proud of herself.

'At least someone's got some good news.' Jack glanced at the main screen for the millionth time.

'I've got even better news.' Slink was sitting in the lounge area with Wren. They were watching cartoons. He stood up and waved his phone at them.

Charlie looked puzzled. 'What's that?'

'One of our other missions.' Slink grinned. 'The trap – it's got something.' He peered at the phone's display. 'And it looks like the right one this time.'

'You have got to be kidding me,' Jack said. 'That thing actually worked?'

Slink nodded. 'Yep.'

'Thanks for having faith in my design,' Charlie grumbled.

'Yeah, right.' Obi frowned. 'You didn't think my camera software would work either?'

'It's not that,' Jack said. 'I just think there's probably a thousand of them and it's not the first time we –'

'Let me see that.' Wren jumped up and Slink handed her the phone. 'That's him,' she said. 'It's *definitely* him.'

'Only one way to be sure.' Slink grabbed his backpack and strode to the dining area.

'You know,' Charlie said to Jack, 'we could go RAKing too. We haven't gone in a while.'

RAKing was Random Acts of Kindness – and they all liked to do it as often as they could. But now wasn't the best time.

'I can't go.' Jack nodded at the screens. 'If the virus comes back –'

'I'll let you know if it does,' Obi said. 'I can watch out for it while you're RAKing.'

Jack sighed. 'I don't know. I'm not really in the mood.'

Slink stuffed postcards into his bag. 'Come on, Jack, it'll be fun.'

Jack looked at Wren – she was bouncing with excitement and doing silent pleading gestures with her hands. Finally, he let out a breath. 'OK, let's go.'

Wren squealed with delight, ran to the airlock door and grabbed her coat from a hook on the wall.

• • •

Mihone Street in East London had the reputation of being one of the worst places in the country to live. High crime. Low income. Everything was dirty and decaying, but most of the residents were just down on their luck. Not given a chance to help themselves.

The Outlaws liked RAKing on Mihone Street – it felt good to put smiles on people's faces.

Jack, Charlie, Slink and Wren marched down an alleyway between an abandoned church and a youth centre.

At the end, Slink lifted a pallet aside to reveal a box underneath, just under a metre square, made out of formed sheet metal.

Charlie stepped back. 'Go for it.'

Wren hurried forward, knelt down and peered

into the box. After a moment, a huge grin swept across her face.

'Well?' Slink said.

She looked up. 'It's him.'

'Get ready.' Slink pressed a button on his phone and the lock on the box disengaged.

Wren lifted the flap, reached inside and carefully took out a cat. It had all black fur apart from a round white patch that covered one ear and half its face.

Slink held up his phone with a picture of the cat filling the display.

Jack looked from the picture to the cat and back again. 'She's right.' He couldn't believe it. The trap they'd made had worked.

Charlie walked over to a skip, rummaged inside and pulled out a cardboard box. She checked it was secure while walking back to Wren. 'We can put him in here,' she said.

Wren was reluctant to let the cat go at first, but then decided it was probably for the best – they didn't want him running off again.

Charlie secured down the flaps. 'Let's take him home,' she said, then the four of them marched from the alley.

As they turned into the road, Obi said in their ears, 'Well? Is it him?'

'Yep,' Slink said. 'We're going there now.'

'Awesome.'

Two roads down, the Outlaws walked into a cul-de-sac. At the end was a rundown terraced house, its garden overgrown and flanked by three-metre high bushes. They stopped outside the gate.

Slink checked the address on his phone and nodded. 'This is the one.'

Charlie held the box out to Wren. 'Do you wanna do it?'

Wren beamed and took it from her.

Slink opened the gate and Wren hurried up the broken path. She reached the front door and gently set the box down on the step. She glanced around, then knocked loudly and ran back down the path.

When she was through the gate, the Outlaws hid behind the bushes and watched.

It was a minute or so before the front door opened and an elderly lady peered out. 'Hello?'

There was a miaowing and clawing sound and she looked at the box. The old lady frowned, then with a lot of effort, she bent down and undid the flaps. She gasped and almost toppled backwards as the cat stuck its head out.

'*Oscar?*' For a long time, the old lady seemed not to believe her eyes.

The cat miaowed again.

The old lady picked Oscar up and cradled him in her arms. 'Where've you been? I was so worried.'

Oscar purred as though nothing was wrong and nuzzled his face into her shoulder.

The old lady's name was Irene Gardener and her cat had been missing for over a month. Some kind neighbours had put up a few posters, but Oscar was nowhere to be seen.

That's when Charlie, Obi, Slink and Wren had come up with the idea of building a trap. Charlie constructed it out of steel, with a flap that would drop into place. They'd set a bowl of tuna as bait and fitted it with a wireless camera.

Every day or two, the trap would go off and Slink would check the pictures. Each time, it had been a different cat, and they'd had to free it and refill the bait. They'd been convinced that Oscar would stay in the local neighbourhood. He just had to stumble upon the box.

'It's a house cat and not used to being outside,' Charlie had said.

'Yeah,' Wren agreed with a fervent nod. 'Oscar is lost, that's all.'

Well, Jack had to hand it to them – they'd been right.

Irene peered in their direction, but they kept out of sight. With another glance up the road, she held Oscar tight, went back inside and shut the door.

Wren smiled. 'That was amazing.'

'Yeah, yeah,' Slink said. 'We can't hang about here all day. We've got things to do.' He pulled a list from his back pocket. 'These are all Wren's ideas today.'

As they walked away, Charlie keyed a message into her phone.

'Who are you texting?' Jack said.

'The Consultant, telling him we've found Oscar.'

'The Consultant' – real name James – was a friend of the Outlaws who helped them out occasionally with missions. This time he'd supplied them with something called the Cat-Cam 9000. Essentially, it was a tiny camera and transmitter which could be inserted into a cat's collar, undetected. Three other cats in the area had been secretly fitted with the cat-cam to pick up images of Oscar.

Charlie's phone beeped. She looked at the display and smiled. 'The Consultant's happy we found him.'

'Me too,' Wren said, skipping after Slink and looking at the list in his hand.

• • •

As always, the next couple of hours passed in a blur.

Slink and Wren had taped money to the back of their homemade postcards and were now handing them out to any homeless person they came across.

Jack and Charlie sauntered behind them as they hurried up and down streets, looking under bridges and in alleyways for worthy recipients.

'Did Obi tell you he's found a plan of another one of his mum and dad's old houses?' Charlie said.

Jack looked at her. 'Another house? How many did his mum and dad have?'

She shrugged. 'They were rich.'

'No kidding.' Jack glanced around and lowered his voice. 'What's he got? Some kind of blueprint?'

She nodded. 'I think so.' She looked thoughtful a moment. 'Obi's really determined to prove his uncle faked his mum and dad's will.'

'Yeah,' Jack said. 'Well, we should have a look at

it. You never know, he might even be right. He was about Proteus, remember?'

Charlie nodded and grinned at him.

'What?' Jack said.

'Nothing. You're just a nice guy. I ever tell you that?'

Jack looked away, embarrassed. 'I'm no saint.'

• • •

Slink and Wren ran out of postcards and the four of them stopped outside a block of flats. First, Wren wanted them to clean up the flowerbeds. Taking it in turns to keep a lookout, they ripped out the weeds, picked up the rubbish and cleaned the stone path.

When they were done, they stood back to admire their handiwork.

'Well?' Jack said to Wren. 'What's next?'

Wren pointed to an underpass by the block of flats. It was almost pitch-black because the flood-light bulb was broken and no one had bothered to fix it. Kids had to walk down that tunnel. It wasn't safe.

They hurried over to it and Wren sat on Charlie's shoulders, unscrewed the glass covering on the light and removed the broken bulb.

'Careful,' Charlie said, passing her a replacement bulb. 'It's mains electricity.'

Wren gingerly took the bulb and clicked it into place.

The light flickered on, illuminating the tunnel.

Wren screwed the cover back and Charlie lowered her to the ground.

Wren stared up at it, looking proud of herself.

Jack's phone beeped. He pulled it from his pocket and looked at the display. It was a text message from Obi.

'What's up?' Charlie asked.

'We have to go home.'

'Why?'

Jack looked at her. 'The program's found the virus.'

• • •

Back at the bunker, they all gathered around Obi's chair.

'I've managed to locate the virus's signal.' Obi clicked a trackerball and brought up a window. 'It's here.'

'Another power station?' Charlie said.

Obi nodded. 'Bransgore – it's in their system.' He

clicked on another window showing the virus's code. 'Looks like it's been there for a couple of hours.'

Jack stared at the monitor as the virus adapted to the new computers it was infecting.

'What's it doing now?' Wren asked.

'If it keeps going like this,' Jack said, 'it could cripple the entire power station. *Permanently.*'

Even take down every power station in the South East. Perhaps the entire country.

The computer beeped and the screen went dark.

Obi's jaw dropped. 'Oh, no.'

'What now?' Charlie said.

'The connection's been severed.'

Jack pulled the keyboard over and started to type quickly. 'He's right.'

'What's "severed"?' Wren asked.

'It means,' Jack said, straightening up, 'the network engineers at Bransgore power station have cut the connection to the internet.' He looked at the others. 'They've done the worst thing possible – they've trapped the virus inside their computer system.'

'Now it's their problem,' Slink said, sipping his lemonade. 'So what?'

'*So,*' Jack took a breath and chose his next words

carefully, 'the virus could cause the power station to have a meltdown.'

They all stared at him.

'Meltdown?' Charlie said. 'You mean it could explode or something?'

Jack shrugged. 'Maybe, yeah.'

'Still don't see the problem,' Slink said.

'That's not all.' Jack turned to the screens and waved a finger. 'If someone gets their hands on the virus, there's a chance they could use it to find us. Track down the location of the bunker.'

'How would they do that?' Obi asked.

'We don't know how this virus works yet,' Jack replied. 'It could be keeping a log of every place it visits.'

'And it's been here before,' Charlie added.

'Exactly,' Jack said, remembering when the virus had infected the bunker's computers and caused havoc.

'What do we do?' Wren asked in a quiet voice.

Jack started to pace, his mind ablaze. 'This is actually the best thing they could've done.'

'Wait,' Slink said. 'A moment ago you were saying –'

Jack stopped. 'They've trapped the virus, right? It has no way out. Don't you see? We can grab it once and for all.' His excitement grew as the realisation dawned on him.

'You're saying we break into that power station?' Charlie said.

Jack nodded. 'We need to remove the virus ourselves. And we need to be quick.'

'How are we going to do that?' Obi asked.

Jack pulled a USB pen drive from his pocket. 'With this.' On the stick was a program he'd used before to send a signal, attracting the virus. If he modified it, he could physically trap the virus.

Slink frowned. 'OK, so how do we get into the power station? They will have some serious security there.'

'I don't know yet,' Jack said. 'But we have to do this. Are you in?'

They all nodded.

'Good.' He turned to Obi. 'Can you hack into all the CCTV cameras around the power station? I need to see what we've got to work with.'

'No problem,' Obi said. 'It's going to take me a while though – I need to find the cameras that aren't affected by the blackouts. If there are any.'

Slink nudged Wren's arm and they went to play on a racing game.

Obi set to work and twenty minutes later he had a

still image from a camera on the other side of the River Thames. It pointed directly at the power station on the opposite bank. Obi zoomed in the image. 'This is the closest I can get.'

Jack pointed at the screen. 'That's where we'll come in – the river side of the plant.'

Obi nodded. 'Looks like the fence is electric, but I bet Slink can get over it.' He glanced at Slink and muttered, 'Hopefully, it'll electrocute him.'

'Obi,' Charlie said, 'play nicely.'

'I'm joking.'

'Is there any way you can see inside the building?' Jack asked.

Obi opened another window. 'No, but I think I can get something else that you can use.'

Jack turned away and watched quietly as Wren beat Slink on the racing game three times in a row.

Finally, Obi said, 'Got it.'

Jack turned back.

Obi gestured at the main monitor. 'I've got you a layout of the inside of the power station.'

Jack leant in. 'Great.' His eyes scanned the architectural plan and he committed it to memory. Finally, he straightened up and looked at Charlie. 'There's not a whole lot of information, but, from what I can see,' he pointed at the image taken from the CCTV camera, 'there's a guard tower and that's where the main security is located. We need to get inside that and patch Obi into their cameras.' He looked over at Slink and Wren.

Wren laughed as she crossed the finishing line for the fourth or fifth time.

Slink swore. 'How do you do that?'

'Guys?' Jack called. They looked back at him. 'We go in thirty minutes.'

Charlie glanced at the time. 'It'll be dark in an hour.'

Jack started pacing back and forth, running different scenarios through his head. He hated not being able to do a recon mission, but they simply didn't have the luxury of time. It was the security services that had built Proteus, the quantum computer, so did that mean they also knew about the virus? If not, it probably wouldn't be long before they found out about it and came to get it themselves.

Now, it was a race.

'Any use for the rapid winch?' Charlie said.

Jack shook his head. 'I don't think we'll need it this time.'

Charlie looked disappointed.

Slink and Wren walked over to them, both

seeming eager to get on with the mission.

'Well?' Slink said to Jack. 'What's the plan? How are we going to break into the power station?'

'You need to get past that fence,' Jack said. 'Then into the tower and connect Obi to their cameras.'

'How?' Charlie said.

'It's a good security system.' Jack looked at the guard tower. 'But it has one major flaw.'

'What's that?'

'The human element. They still use a guard in that tower to monitor it. That's the weak point.' Jack smiled. 'That's the way in.'

'Right,' Slink said. 'But how do we get to the fence in the first place? In case you haven't noticed, the River Thames is on the other side of it.'

Jack took a deep breath and looked at Charlie. He was going to regret this, but he had no other ideas. 'Is Stingray still running?'

Charlie stared at him. 'Are you sure you want to use it? You remember what happened the last time?'

Jack sighed. 'No, I'm not sure, but it's the best solution I have.'

Slink let out a whoop, which made everyone jump. 'This is gonna be freakin cool,' he shouted. 'I love Stingray.'

CHAPTER FOUR

AN HOUR LATER, JACK WAS SITTING HUNCHED
over, with his knees to his chest, wishing he'd been able to think of another way to do this. The air was so hot that he was finding it hard to breathe.

Wren was sitting directly behind him, curled up in a similar position. In front of Jack was Slink, and in front of him was Charlie.

So, here they were, the four of them crammed into this steel tube, sweating like mad and rapidly running out of oxygen.

Fan-tastic.

Jack shuffled his weight, trying to ease the stiffness in his legs.

On top of everything else, the constant hum of the electric motor reverberating off the metal walls was really beginning to annoy him.

They'd 'acquired' Stingray – the small submarine –

from some weapons smugglers the year before. The smugglers had been using it to transport guns into the United Kingdom. Jack's first instinct was to destroy the sub, but Charlie had managed to persuade him that it could be useful to them.

Now Jack wished he hadn't listened to her.

They called the submarine Stingray because of a sticker of the fish they'd found above the control dashboard.

'Are we there yet?' Slink asked for the millionth time.

Over Slink's shoulder, Jack could see Charlie with her face pressed against a periscope that disappeared through the ceiling above her head. In front of her were a couple of displays that shone blue and gave her skin an ethereal glow.

Charlie had a joystick in her hand. 'You ask me that one more time, Slink,' she said through tight lips, 'and I'll open the hatch right here.'

'Whatever,' Slink said. 'I'd rather swim anyway.'

Me too, Jack thought. But the strong current would probably drown them all. Besides, he also knew how dirty the water in the Thames was and the likelihood of them catching some incurable disease was even more probable.

・ ・ ・

After what seemed like an eternity, the thrum of the motor finally eased.

'We're there,' Charlie said. 'Surfacing.'

'Thank God.' Slink half turned. 'Jack?'

'What?'

'You may have to shove me from behind. My bum cheeks have gone to sleep and I don't think they'll ever wake up.'

'Breaking the surface,' Charlie said with obvious annoyance.

Stingray punched through the water, rocked from side to side, then stabilised.

Slink scooted forward, reached into an opening above his head and turned a large wheel.

It squeaked, making Jack wince.

Finally, Slink pushed the hatch upward and glorious fresh oxygen flooded the tube.

Jack pulled in big lungfuls of the cold air as Slink's feet disappeared up through the hatch.

Charlie motioned for him to go next.

Grateful, Jack edged forward and stood up. He put his hands on either side of the hatch and lifted himself into the night air.

Charlie had guided Stingray to the exact location of Bransgore power station. They were next to a high fence and at the top of each section was a red light. Beyond the fence was the power station itself.

A fine rain dusted their clothes and Jack braced his feet, careful not to slip.

He pulled up his hood and bandana and looked around.

Lights from the city reflected off the dark water of the Thames and blinked on and off, which meant the virus was still hard at work infecting the power supply.

'Hey.'

Jack glanced down to see a disgruntled Wren looking back at him. She stretched her arms up. He helped her out of the hatch and on to the top deck of the submarine. Next, Charlie clambered out, and the four of them adjusted their bandanas and hoods, making sure their faces were hidden, and they sat in silence.

Jack pulled his mini binoculars from his pocket and pressed them to his eyes. First, he looked at the main security tower. He could make out the guard through the window, sat in there with his back to them. Jack then quickly scanned the outside of the power station building, looking for extra security cameras, but could only see the one above the emergency exit.

That was the thing about security engineers, he thought. *They were overconfident*. Obviously, the designer of this place had decided not to use many external cameras because he or she felt no one would ever get over the fence and past the guard tower.

Jack smiled inwardly. That designer hadn't banked on two things. One – that the electricity supply to the fence would be going on and off. And two – they'd never heard of the Urban Outlaws.

The light in the guard tower was the only one that wasn't blinking on and off. Its power was isolated and running from a generator buried deep within the main building. This also powered the cameras and they too were on an internal system. So, the Outlaws had to get into the tower, disable the guard and take over the security.

Simple.

Jack scanned the side of the tower. The walls were made of smooth concrete and there was no way to climb up.

At ground level was a door. Jack focused on the

lock – it was a keypad. 'It's like we thought,' he said, handing Charlie the binoculars. 'We definitely can't get past it, right?'

Charlie peered through the binoculars and shook her head. 'It's coded and linked to the security console in the tower. We mess with it and the guard will know.'

'OK,' Jack said. 'There's only one way to do this then.' He looked down at the base of the fence but could see it was anchored into the concrete with large steel hooks.

Definitely no way under it.

'You think you can make it over?' he said to Slink. It looked a lot higher and imposing up close.

'Of course.' Slink stood and rubbed his hands together, obviously eager to get on with his latest challenge.

Much to Jack's relief, the fence was powering down with the electricity supply that ran parts of the city. The bright red light on each section blinked on and off. The only problem was it seemed random, with no discernible pattern to it.

'Why isn't the fence on the same power as the guard tower?' Slink said.

'Needs too much juice,' Charlie said. 'They've

kept the cameras and control systems connected to the generator, but the fence is linked to the main power station.'

Another mistake the designer had made, thought Jack.

There was a further problem, however – with most electric fences you had to be standing on the ground and gripping the wires if it was going to electrocute you. But not with this one – the wires alternated live and neutral horizontally going up, separated by plastic spacers. So, if you tried to climb it, it was more than likely that your feet would be on a live wire while your hands were gripping a neutral one, thus completing the circuit and giving you a nasty electric shock. Sure, Slink could try to stand on a neutral wire while gripping another one, avoiding a live wire, but they were so close together, it was nearly impossible, especially in the dark.

Charlie suggested trying to short the fence so that the power would be permanently down and Slink could get over it that way, but Jack pointed out that it wouldn't take the guard long to realise the lights on the fence weren't switching on with the rest of the power.

No, the only chance Slink had was to just hurry up

and make it over before the power came back on again. The rain made the wires even more treacherous, so that wouldn't be easy.

Slink's lips moved, silently counting each time the electricity went off.

Jack did the same. The first count was thirty-two seconds. The second time the electricity went off for only twenty seconds. The third time lasted for almost forty seconds.

Jack glanced up. Even that didn't seem long enough.

Slink cracked his knuckles.

'Well?' Jack said. 'The shortest time so far is twenty seconds. Can you do it?'

Slink shrugged. 'I think so.'

Charlie frowned at him. 'You *think* so?' She looked anxious and glanced at Jack.

Perhaps we should call it off, Jack thought. As he stared at Charlie, she too seemed unsure what to do.

Wren gasped.

Jack wheeled around to see Slink was already on the fence and climbing.

Jack counted off the seconds –

Five.

Ten.

Slink was not even halfway to the top yet. At this rate, Jack gauged he'd need a lot more time than twenty seconds.

Fifteen seconds.

Twenty seconds . . .

Slink was still a couple of metres from the top and climbing as fast as he could.

Jack ground his teeth – *twenty-five seconds* – and his eyes narrowed to slits.

Slink's feet slipped off the wet wires. He fell a metre or so but managed to get a grip with his hands.

Charlie and Wren went rigid, their eyes wide.

Thirty seconds.

Slink regained his foothold and continued to scramble up the fence.

Jack's forehead felt wet. He wasn't sure if it was the rain or sweat.

Thirty five seconds and the light at the top of the fence came on. Slink held on to it with his hands, but left his feet dangling in mid-air so as not to touch the electric wires.

Jack allowed a small sigh of relief, but Slink still had to get down the other side.

For a full forty seconds the light remained firmly on.

'You're OK, Slink,' Charlie said, though she didn't sound so convinced.

Finally, the light went out again.

Slink made a move to step on the wires when the light suddenly came back on.

'No way,' Jack hissed. 'That was only a couple of seconds.'

Slink looked down at them. 'What now?'

The light seemed to stay on for ages before it finally turned off again.

Slink didn't hang about – in less than fifteen seconds he was on the ground on the other side of the fence.

He grinned at the others and gave them a thumbs-up.

'Nice one,' Jack whispered.

Slink glanced around and then – keeping low – hurried towards the guard tower. He reached the door at the base and looked up. It was a sheer wall, ten metres high. Above the door was a narrow roof that Slink could use.

'Just like we said,' Jack whispered into his microphone. 'From the plan, it looks like the keypad lock on the door is linked to the guard's security terminal.'

Slink knelt down, rubbed his hands on the wet grass and flicked water over the keypad.

'What's he doing?' Wren said.

'Making it look like rain is getting on the keypad and shorting out the circuit,' Jack said. 'It'll buy him the time he needs.'

Slink flicked water on the keypad twice more before typing in a code.

The light above the keypad turned red.

'First wrong code.' Jack glanced up at the guard. He hadn't moved.

'What's Slink doing?' Wren said, wringing her hands.

'Three wrong attempts and a warning will trigger on the guard's console,' Charlie said.

Slink typed a second set of numbers and the keypad's red light came on again, but the guard still hadn't risen from his seat.

Slink pulled back and looked at the others.

'One more time,' Charlie said, into her headset.

Slink nodded and typed in a third code.

Jack watched as the guard looked at something in front of him, then got out of his chair and

85

disappeared from view as he descended the steps inside to come and take a look.

Jack waved at Slink. 'Go.' He, Charlie and Wren crouched down on the sub, staying out of view.

Slink jumped up and gripped the roof above the doorframe, then hauled himself on to it.

The door opened and a guard peered out. He flicked on a torch, took a couple of steps forward and scanned the area.

Slink silently lowered himself to the ground behind the guard, backed into the tower and pulled the door closed.

The guard spun around, rushed to the door and rattled the handle, but it was locked. He cursed to himself and looked at the keypad.

Meanwhile, Jack could make out Slink up in the tower.

'I'm here, Obi,' came his urgent whisper over the headset.

'Hook me in,' Obi said.

Slink ducked below the window.

He was now planting a wireless USB stick that Obi could use to hack into the power station's security systems.

Jack glanced back at the base of the tower. The

guard was wiping rain from the keypad with his sleeve.

'Hurry up, guys,' Jack said into his headset.

'It's in,' Slink said.

'On it.' Obi's voice sounded calm, but then suddenly changed. 'Oh, no.'

'What?' Jack said.

'They've got internal firewalls.'

'Use the Dragon program I wrote.'

'Give me a second.'

Jack glanced back at the tower just as the door closed. 'Too late. Slink, the guard's on his way back.'

Slink's head popped up and he looked around, obviously weighing up his options.

'Obi, hurry,' Jack said. 'Cut the lights.'

'I can't. I'm not in yet. They're well protected.'

Time was up.

Slink ran to the window, opened it and climbed out.

Jack tensed. This was not the plan.

Slink pushed the window closed and hauled himself on to the roof, his feet disappearing just as the guard stepped back into the tower room.

'Oh, brilliant,' Charlie muttered. She turned to Jack. 'I bet you wish I'd brought the rapid winch now, huh?'

The guard sat down at the computer console.

Obi said, 'I'm in. Right, let's see what we've got to play with.'

'Take your time, big guy.' Slink sat cross-legged on the roof, seemingly resigned to his fate.

There had to be a way to get him down from there, but in order to do so, they had to get the guard out of that tower again.

Jack's mind turned over the options.

'OK,' Obi said. 'I've found it.'

The light above the electric fence was still blinking on and off.

'Are you sure?' Charlie said.

'One hundred per cent,' Obi said. 'I've isolated the lights from the fence's main power. You're good to go.'

Charlie stepped forward and stretched out her hand. She glanced at Jack, then tapped one of the wires. Nothing happened so she tapped another one. Finally satisfied the power was definitely off, Charlie slid a pair of bolt cutters out of her bag and set to work cutting the wires.

Jack looked up at Slink. 'Just stay there. I'm still thinking.'

Slink adjusted his hood and crossed his arms. 'I'm not going anywhere.'

'And I'm guessing there're no anchor points?' Jack said.

Slink glanced around. 'Nope.'

'That's going to be a problem.'

Slink bowed his head. 'Ace.'

Jack looked at Charlie – she was still cutting through the fence.

Suddenly, Jack had an idea. He turned to Wren.

'What?' she said, noticing his expression.

Jack glanced back up at the tower. 'Slink, is there anywhere to brace your feet?'

Slink looked around and said, 'Yeah. Why?'

'Do you think you could lift Wren up to you?'

There was a short pause, then Slink said, 'Sure, but what's the point of us both being stuck up here?'

'I have a plan. Get ready, OK?'

Slink slipped off his backpack and pulled out a coil of rope.

'Make sure the guard doesn't see it,' Jack said. 'Feed the rope down between the windows.'

'Ready.' Charlie had cut the fence and folded back the wires, making a big hole.

Jack, Charlie and Wren ducked through the fence and sprinted to the base of the tower.

'OK,' Jack whispered. 'We need to time this right.'

He grabbed the end of Slink's rope and tied it securely around Wren's waist. Jack spoke quietly into his headset. 'Slink, haul her up to you. Understood?'

'Understood,' came the reply.

Jack turned to Wren. 'Use your feet to keep yourself steady, stop yourself spinning and make sure the guard doesn't spot you.'

Wren held tightly on to the rope as Slink lifted her.

'Hey, Wren,' Slink said through heavy breaths. 'What have you been eating? You weigh a ton.'

Wren giggled.

'Pack it in,' Jack said. 'The guard will hear you.'

When Wren was safely on the roof with Slink, Jack and Charlie hurried back to the fence and crouched down.

'Slink,' Jack said. 'I want Wren to execute Operation Handshake. Then you drop down the other side of the tower to her, understood?'

There was a short pause, then Slink said, 'This is going to be funny.' He pulled a penknife from his pocket and started cutting the rope, while explaining the plan to Wren.

'Tell me when you're ready.' Jack stared at the guard – who was completely oblivious to what was going on above him.

A minute later, Slink had cut the rope into two halves, tied knots and said, 'We're good to go.'

Jack took a deep breath. 'Count to five and lower her down.'

'Jack,' Charlie whispered, 'if he drops her –'

'He won't,' Jack said, but his stomach knotted with anxiety anyway.

'Five.' Slink braced his feet against the edge of the roof and held on to Wren's rope. 'Four.'

Wren was grinning as though she was going to enjoy this.

'Three.'

Jack glanced at Charlie. She was biting her nails.

'Two.'

Slink redoubled his grip. *'One.'* He lowered Wren down.

Suddenly, she appeared directly in front of the guard's station.

At first he didn't notice her.

Wren thrashed about as though she was panicking.

The guard's eyes snapped up and his gaze locked on to her. He dropped his sandwich, leapt from his chair, reached over to the window and opened it.

'Help me,' Wren screamed, and held out her hand.

The guard grabbed hold of it in both of his, went to pull her inside, but Wren slipped the second rope around his wrists and yanked it tight, so he could no longer move them.

'Now,' Wren shouted, and she held on to the window frame as Slink released her rope, grabbed the end of the rope that was attached to the guard's wrists and leapt off the other side of the tower.

The guard shouted in pain as he was pulled halfway out of the window.

Wren hauled herself over him, ran across the room and opened the opposite window.

Slink clambered through and quickly tied the end of the guard's rope around a stair rail.

The guard shouted as he struggled to pull himself back into the tower, but it was no use – the rope tying his wrists was too tight.

Slink removed his bandana and, with a lot of effort, managed to gag the guard's mouth with it. He then gestured for Wren to let the others in. Jack and Charlie ran to the base of the tower. Wren opened the door and they quickly slipped inside.

As they passed Wren, Charlie smiled at her. 'That was awesome.'

Jack reached the top of the stairs, walked over to the guard and unclipped a set of keys from his belt. 'Right,' he said, turning back to Slink and Wren. 'You two stay here. Keep an eye on him and look out for more guards. Let us know if you spot any trouble.' He turned to the stairs.

'Wait,' Slink said. 'Shouldn't I come with you?'

'No,' Jack said. 'The more of us who go in, the higher the risk of being caught.'

The guard struggled again and almost toppled out of the window.

'Careful,' Slink said. 'I'm not sure the rope can take your weight.'

The guard's shoulders slumped as he realised there was no escape.

Jack and Charlie hurried down the stairs and back into the compound. Keeping low, they sprinted over to the emergency exit of the main building.

'Obi?' Jack said into his headset microphone. 'Is it clear?'

'Yes,' Obi said. 'The engineers and other guards are in the main control room. The corridors are empty.'

Jack unlocked the door with the guard's keys, gestured Charlie through and they crept inside.

They moved along a narrow corridor with fluorescent light strips every few metres. Thick pipes ran along the walls and ceiling.

Jack and Charlie reached a T-junction at the end. The lights flickered on and off.

'Which way?' Charlie whispered.

Jack unclipped his torch and looked left – that way led to the main control room and according to Obi that was the last place they wanted to be.

Jack closed his eyes and visualised the plan of the power station that he'd committed to memory. When he was sure which way they had to go – he opened his eyes again and pointed down the right-hand corridor.

Charlie nodded and they jogged along it.

They took several turns, went down a short flight of steps, then ran along another hallway.

It was like a maze, made even more confusing by the lights constantly flickering off and on.

At the end of the next hallway, they stopped outside an unmarked door.

Charlie took the guard's keys from Jack. 'I hope you know your way out of here.'

'So do I.' Jack gave her a weak smile.

Charlie found the right key and opened the door.

Jack glanced around and followed her inside.

The room beyond was ten metres on each side and very hot. Fans from server cabinets whirred. Jack stared at them and wondered if they ran that hot normally, or was it the virus at work? He imagined it moving through the network wires like sickness through the veins of a diseased animal.

He scanned the room. There were thick power cables disappearing through the wall. Obviously, the computers ran on their own isolated supply – probably the same generator that fed the tower.

That was a huge mistake, Jack thought. It would have been better if the computers had been shut down. That way the virus wouldn't do any more damage.

He spotted a terminal jutting out from one of the cabinets and he and Charlie hurried over to it.

A network cable hung loose from the hub, where the techies had severed the link to the outside world to prevent more damage. Now the virus had nowhere to escape to – but that was just what Jack needed to put a stop to this once and for all.

He pulled out the USB stick with his program on it and plugged it into the main terminal. 'I hope this works.'

Charlie nodded. 'So do I.'

Jack smiled.

A pop-up box appeared on the screen.

'Guys?' It was Obi.

They both froze.

'What's wrong?' Jack said.

'We've got trouble. There's a –'

A crackling sound made Jack wince.

He pulled the headset away from his ear for a moment and said, 'Obi? You there?'

No answer.

'Obi?'

Still no answer.

The connection had been lost.

Jack looked at Charlie.

'What's going on?' she said. 'Power cuts again?'

'I don't know.' Jack had one of his bad feelings. 'Let's get this sorted and get out of here.'

He typed a quick command into the terminal and his program started to send out a signal to the virus.

'Is it working?' Charlie said.

Jack nodded. The virus had taken the bait and was now flowing to his USB stick. In a couple of minutes, they'd have it.

They heard hurried footfall coming from the hall-way.

Jack cursed and glanced around the room. There was nowhere to hide.

He looked at the USB. Its red light blinked as the virus transferred to it.

The footsteps sounded louder now – there wasn't any time left.

Jack grabbed a coffee coaster from next to the keyboard and rested it over the USB stick, hiding the flashing red light.

He pulled his hand back and spun around just as the door burst open. Three men stood in the door-way. Two were guards; the other had a name badge that read 'Night Duty Manager'.

He stepped forward and snarled, 'Look what we have here.'

CHAPTER FIVE

THE NIGHT DUTY MANAGER AND THE TWO GUARDS escorted Jack and Charlie down a winding corridor, with the lights flickering on and off all the while. Unfortunately, they never went out long enough for Jack and Charlie to make a run for it. That, coupled with the fact that one of the guards had Jack's shoulder in a painful grip, made an escape impossible.

It also seemed to Jack that the power outages were becoming more frequent. At least he knew his program was working hard at capturing the virus, even if they didn't know how they were going to retrieve the USB stick once it had done its job.

As they walked, the night duty manager said, 'Is all this your fault? The power?'

Jack glanced at Charlie and then at the guards. 'How can it be *our* fault? We've only just got here.'

The man snarled. 'And what exactly were you two doing?'

'We got split up from our tour group,' Charlie said, with a huge measure of sarcasm.

The night duty manager's eyes narrowed. 'Funny kid.' He reached over and yanked both of their hoods and bandanas down. 'Now the real reason.'

Jack tried his best to appear innocent. 'We were just having a look around. We saw the power kept going on and off, so we sneaked in. We're urban explorers.'

'Try again, sunshine,' the night duty manager said. 'I wasn't born yesterday.'

Jack realised they were not going to be able to talk their way out of this. He wondered if Obi had seen what had happened and told Slink and Wren. Would they escape before the other guards went to investigate? Jack hoped they'd all got away.

At the end of the hallway, the guards stopped, removed Jack and Charlie's backpacks and threw them to the floor.

'Hey,' Charlie shouted. 'Be careful with my stuff.'

The guards opened a door and shoved them inside.

The night duty manager turned to one guard. 'Wait here.' He looked at Jack and Charlie. 'The police will deal with you.' He motioned for the other guard to follow him.

The remaining guard smirked and slammed the door shut.

The lock clicked.

Jack stared at the door, then spun around.

They were in a small room lined with shelves, each crammed full of cleaning supplies.

Jack looked for an escape route. There was only a small ventilation grate – no way in there, and the suspended ceiling didn't look strong enough to take their weight anyway.

There were no other doors.

No windows.

Jack tried his headset again, but Obi still didn't respond. He looked at Charlie. 'We're trapped.'

'Mm-hmm.' Charlie moved along the shelves, muttering under her breath.

The lights went out.

Jack reached into his pocket, pulled out his torch and flicked it on.

'Give me that,' Charlie said, taking it from him and turning back to the shelves.

'What are you doing?'

'Reading.'

Jack frowned at her. 'Reading what?'

Charlie picked up a white bottle with a red skull and crossbones emblazoned on it. 'Labels.' She grabbed another, smaller, green bottle. 'Hold these.'

Jack took them from her.

Finally, Charlie removed a large black bottle and a bucket from the bottom shelf. She put the bucket in the corner of the room, opened the black bottle and upended it.

The *glug, glug* of the green liquid smelt like pine disinfectant.

Once emptied, Charlie tossed the bottle aside and motioned for Jack to hand her the other two.

She rechecked the labels, opened the white bottle and tipped half of its contents into the bucket. This one smelt like bleach mixed with alcohol.

Jack screwed his nose up and took a step back as it started to hiss.

Charlie opened the last bottle and hesitated. 'We need a few other things first.' She set the bottle down and refocused her attention on the shelves.

After a moment, she opened a pack of cleaning cloths and tossed two of them to Jack.

'What are these for?'

Charlie pointed to a mop and bucket by the door. 'Dip them in that water.'

Jack walked over and peered inside.

There were hair and leaves floating in it. 'It's not exactly clean water, Charlie,' he said, screwing his nose up at the brown liquid.

'Just do it,' Charlie said. 'What do you want? Mineral water?'

Reluctantly, Jack dipped the cloths in the dirty liquid.

When he was done, Charlie took one of them from him and returned to the other bucket.

'Right,' she said. 'This might not work.'

'What exactly are you doing?'

Charlie pointed to the ceiling directly above her. There was a fire alarm – its red light blinking.

Jack looked at the bucket. 'You're gonna set it off with the chemicals?'

She nodded. 'You might want to put that over your nose and mouth.'

Jack stared at the wet cloth. Yellow-brown water dripped to the floor. 'Put it over my mouth?' he said, incredulous. 'Are you kidding me?'

Charlie held her own cloth in one hand and the

bottle poised over the bucket in the other. 'I'm not sure how toxic this will be.'

'Toxic?' Jack said. 'Is this likely to cause any *permanent* damage to us?'

Charlie looked at the bucket, the bottle in her hand and then considered him for a moment. 'Maybe.'

'Great,' Jack said. 'Let's just call for an ambulance now. Wait.' He glanced at the locked door. 'How are you so sure that guard will open it?'

'I'm not.' Charlie upended the bottle.

The liquid in the bucket immediately started bubbling and fumes poured into the air in a billowing plume.

The stench of chemicals made Jack gag.

Reluctantly, he held the wet cloth over his mouth and nose. The smell of dirt and cleaning fluid wasn't much better.

The bucket continued to pour out grey smoke-like vapour.

Charlie wafted it towards the fire alarm and she stepped back, her own cloth pressed to her face.

For an agonising minute or so, nothing happened and the room filled up with more of the acrid fumes. It stung Jack's eyes and he squinted up at the fire alarm.

Was it even working?

He could barely see the blinking red LED now.

Jack and Charlie both started coughing.

Finally, just when Jack thought he was going to pass out, the alarm sounded, piercing the quietness.

He heard the guard swear loudly outside the door and fumble with a set of keys.

Jack felt dizzy and had to steady himself against the wall.

Charlie grabbed two bottles of washing-up liquid from the shelf and tossed one to him.

Jack frowned at it. 'What's this for?'

The door opened and Charlie burst through, knocking the guard aside, catching him off balance.

Jack ran after her, chucked the cloth away and bent double, coughing and gasping for air.

Surprised, the guard staggered back as the fumes billowed into the hallway. 'What have you two done?'

Without a word, Charlie scooped her bag up off the floor and ran.

Jack stood stunned for a second, then grabbed his own bag and sprinted after her, with the guard hard on his heels.

'Stop!'

When Jack caught up with Charlie, she popped the lid off the washing-up liquid and squirted it on to the floor behind them.

Jack immediately did the same and they took a right, sprinting down another corridor.

There was a shout of pain.

Jack glanced back.

The guard had tried to round the corner, but had slammed into the opposite wall. He was now struggling to get his balance. He tried to run after them, but fell flat on his back and let out another roar.

Jack and Charlie carried on running until they reached a T-junction.

'Which way?' Charlie said.

They had to go back and grab the USB drive from the computer room.

Jack visualised the floor plan of the power station in his mind. 'Left.' He glanced at her. 'I think.'

They hurried off in that direction, moving as fast as they could. They didn't want to get caught a second time.

Finally, they reached the computer room and sneaked inside. The program must have worked and the virus was on Jack's USB drive.

Jack's feet slipped. He looked down. 'Why's the floor wet in here?'

'Probably from the guards' boots.' Charlie hurried over to the terminal. 'No.'

'What's wrong?' Jack said.

She pointed at the empty USB slot. 'Where is it?'

Jack's breath caught. 'I left it there.' He glanced up at the camera in the corner of the room. Could Obi see them? 'The guards,' he said. 'They must have taken it.' Jack hurried over to the terminal and started to type. 'The virus has definitely gone from their system.'

Charlie frowned. 'Which means it's on your drive, right? We need to find out what they've done with it.'

They heard shouts coming from down the corridor.

'We have to go,' Jack said. He plugged the network cable into the back of the terminal and made a mental note of the IP address.

They then both crept into the hallway.

The shouting was coming from their left. Jack and Charlie ran right, following the twists and turns of the corridor, up the steps, and back outside.

As they sprinted to the fence, Jack glanced up.

The guard was still hanging out of the window and his cold eyes followed them.

Slink held the wire on the fence open and Wren was already climbing into the sub.

Charlie ducked through the hole.

'We heard the alarms and shouting,' Slink said. 'What happened?'

The emergency-exit door banged open and the two guards and night duty manager ran outside. They stopped and looked around.

'Let's get out of here.' Jack ducked through the fence and gestured for Charlie and Slink to get into the submarine.

As they clambered through Stingray's hatch, the night duty manager caught sight of Jack and for a second he seemed puzzled. It was probably the first time he'd seen a mini submarine bobbing on the surface of the River Thames.

He quickly came to his senses, however, and started running towards the fence. 'There,' he shouted at the guards.

Jack swung his legs over the hole and dropped into the sub. He closed the hatch, spun the wheel and sat down.

There was a sudden loud *thunk* above them.

'What was that?' Wren said.

Charlie pressed her eyes to the periscope. 'That dozy idiot has just jumped onboard.' Her fingers moved over the controls.

There was a squeak above Jack's head. He looked up and gasped – the wheel to the hatch was turning. Jack grabbed hold of it. 'Quick, Charlie.'

'Diving.'

Jack struggled to keep the hatch secured. The wheel moved a couple of centimetres as the man above fought to undo it. 'Hurry up.' Jack's arms strained as the wheel turned a few more centimetres. The guy was too strong for him.

Suddenly, the pressure on the wheel eased and Jack secured it back into place.

'It's OK,' Charlie said, looking through the periscope. 'He's gone for a swim.'

As they dived to the bottom of the Thames, Jack spoke into his headset. 'Obi, can you hear us now?'

'Yes.'

'Please tell me you recorded all the CCTV cameras?'

'Of course.'

Jack let out a small breath. He could always rely

on Obi. 'And you've got a recording for the computer room?'

'Yeah, I've got it.'

'Great,' Jack said. 'I want you to watch that recording from the moment Charlie and I went in there.'

'I don't need to,' Obi said. 'I was watching it all happen.'

There was something about Obi's voice that was unsettling.

'So,' Jack said. 'What did happen?'

'Just come home,' Obi said. 'I'll get the recordings ready for you.'

Jack didn't like the sound of that.

• • •

An hour and a half later, they were back in the bunker.

Jack hurried over to Obi. 'Any idea which one of the guards took my USB stick?'

Obi nodded. 'Yeah. None of them.'

'What do you mean?'

Obi clicked on the screen. 'It wasn't a guard that found it.' He brought up an image of the computer room and sped the recording forward.

Jack watched as he and Charlie entered, plugged in the USB stick, then were caught and escorted out by the guards.

Obi fast-forwarded a couple more minutes and paused it. 'Watch this.' He hit play.

The time and date counter ticked off in the corner of the screen.

The lights in the room periodically went off and on.

The door to the computer room opened and a hooded figure stepped inside.

'Who's that?' Slink said.

The person lowered their hood, glanced up at the camera and they all got a clear look at his face. He was a boy, no older than Jack and Charlie – fourteen, maybe fifteen. He had an olive complexion, with dark, almost black, hair, and he wore a backpack.

Charlie leant into the display. 'He looks like one of us.'

'Why's he wet?' Wren said.

She was right – the kid's clothes were dripping water all over the floor.

Charlie glanced at Jack, but she didn't need to say anything.

He nodded – the floor had been wet when they went back to retrieve the USB stick.

The kid moved to the computer terminal, typed something in, then reached over and pulled out the USB drive. After examining it for a moment, he undid his jacket and slid it into an inner pocket.

'Little thief,' Slink said.

The kid glanced around and left the server room.

Jack looked at the time on the screen. It had taken the kid less than a minute to steal their drive. He sighed. 'Looks like someone had the same idea as us.'

Obi scanned through the recordings and found one from the camera on the other side of the Thames.

The five of them watched the monitor.

'There,' Jack said, pointing.

The water rippled by the submarine and a head popped up. For a while, it bobbed there, obviously assessing the situation.

Obi zoomed the image in the best he could. 'He's wearing a mask and snorkel.'

'Guess he also had a wetsuit on under his clothes,' Charlie said. 'How did he not drown? The current is –'

'Look,' Wren said.

They all leant into the screen as Obi paused the image.

'What is that?' Slink said.

The kid was gripping on to a black cylinder about half a metre in length.

Charlie made a sound somewhere between a gasp and a squeak. 'I've always wanted one of those.'

'What is it?' Obi said.

'A DPV. They're amazing. Cost a fortune.'

'What's a DPV?'

'A Diver Propulsion Vehicle.' Noticing everyone's blank expressions, Charlie continued. 'It's like an underwater scooter. Divers use it to get around. It has a motor that drags you along.'

'What's the range?' Jack said.

Charlie shrugged. 'Depends on the model. Two or three miles.'

'So, he could've come from anywhere.' Jack looked at the main display as Obi hit the Play button again.

The kid stopped next to the submarine, pulled himself out of the water and slipped through the hole in the fence they'd cut.

He crouched down, slipped off his mask and snorkel, and tucked them into his backpack.

He glanced at the submarine, then up at the tower.

'Now he's seen you two,' Obi said to Slink and Wren. 'How did you not spot him?'

As if in answer, the kid pulled up his hood and sprang forward. Keeping low, he sprinted to the base of the tower.

'He's fast,' Charlie said.

Slink crossed his arms and muttered, 'Not that fast.'

The kid waited there a second, with his back pressed against the wall, then, with another quick look around, he sprinted to the emergency exit, opened the door and went inside the building.

Obi brought up another file that showed the camera view from the hallway and matched the time stamp. 'Watch between the blackouts,' he said, and hit Play.

The kid took a few steps into the corridor, pulled a device from his bag and pressed it high on the wall.

'That's when I saw him and tried to tell you,' Obi said.

'When we were in the computer room.' Jack frowned at the kid's device, then looked at Charlie. 'Phone signal blocker?'

She nodded.

The image went dark, and when it came back on again, the kid was gone.

'I'll show you what happened when he left.' Obi opened another recording and they watched the kid run back out of the building, past the guard tower and stop at the fence. He put on his mask and snorkel, ducked through the hole and slipped beneath the surface of the water.

'Obi, can you go back to the time he was in the computer room?' Jack said. 'I want to see something.'

Obi clicked the trackerball and the recording appeared on the screen.

Jack leant in, watching as the kid typed.

'There's no way we can tell what he's typing,' Obi said.

'There is a way.' Jack pointed. 'Look at his fingers.'

If they were lucky, they'd be able to work out what keys he was pressing.

'Is that a "Q"?' Wren asked.

'No,' Obi said. 'It's numbers. I'm sure of it.'

Jack nodded as he watched. Obi sped the recording back and then forward again. He was right – the kid was definitely typing numbers.

Suddenly, it dawned on Jack. 'It's an IP address,' he said. 'The kid was checking the computers, looking for the virus. See?' He pointed at the kid as he stopped typing. 'Now he realises it's transferred to my USB stick.'

Sure enough – the kid removed it and slid it into his pocket.

'So,' Obi said, 'he has the virus now?'

Jack straightened up. 'Yep. We need to find him, get the virus and put an end to this.' He took the keyboard from Obi and set to work.

'Let's give Jack some space.' Charlie signalled to Slink and Wren, and the three of them walked to the kitchen to make snacks.

First, Jack checked Bransgore's computers were connected to the internet again. They were, so he hacked into them and opened the logs. The records showed the kid had first looked in the main system for the virus, then followed the path to Jack's USB drive. Jack was impressed – the kid knew what he was doing.

But he'd made one mistake – he'd taken Jack's

program with him, not just the virus, but the whole thing.

In every piece of code Jack wrote, he included a homing beacon in case it was stolen. It was a way for Jack to locate and recover his own software, should anything like this happen.

The homing beacon broadcast a unique finger-print that Jack could use to track it.

He set a trace program running, but had no way of knowing how long it would take for the kid to plug the USB drive into a computer that was connected to the internet.

Jack handed the keyboard back to Obi and sighed. Now it was only a matter of time. He just hoped they caught up with the kid before the virus escaped again.

CHAPTER SIX

THE NEXT MORNING, JACK WAS LEANING AGAINST Obi's chair, with the keyboard and tracker-ball pulled towards him as he stared at the screen. Every hour he'd woken up and come to check to see if his program had traced the kid. This time, he decided to stay and work on something else while he waited.

The door behind Jack opened and Obi waddled in, rubbing his eyes. 'Have you been up all night?'

Jack yawned. 'Most of it.'

Obi climbed into his chair. 'What's that?' He pointed at a series of seemingly random letters and numbers on the screen.

'It's called *Kryptos*.'

'Some sort of secret code?' Obi asked.

'Yeah.'

'And you've cracked it?'

'Maybe, I don't know.' Jack closed a few of the windows and pushed the keyboard and trackerball to Obi. 'It seems to start with, "All free men". But, I haven't finished the –'

Suddenly, there was a beeping sound.

'No way,' Jack said. 'That's just typical.'

Obi clicked the trackerball. 'It's the trace program. We've got him.'

Jack took the keyboard back from Obi and typed. After checking and rechecking where the signal was coming from, he said, 'Can you call the others?'

A minute later, Charlie rushed over, followed by Slink and Wren. 'What's going on?'

'We've found the kid.' Jack spun the monitor round so they could all see it. It showed a map of London with a blinking red dot over a building next to Covent Garden. 'He's there.'

They all leant in for a better look.

Charlie frowned. 'Jack, are you sure that's right?'

'Positive. Now watch this.' Jack hacked straight into the kid's computer and opened his email account. 'His name's Hector.'

'Guess he's a hacker too,' Slink said.

Jack nodded. 'He seems pretty good at it. His IP and MAC addresses are well masked, and he's using several proxies. Unfortunately for him, my program's beacon cut right through all his defences.'

'I've seen that name before,' Obi said. 'He was on the Cerberus forum a while back. He's the guy that hacked into that supermarket computer and changed all their prices.' Obi looked at Jack. 'You remember? Everything in the shop cost a penny?'

'Bet you loved that,' Slink said.

Obi scowled at him and continued, 'It caused mayhem – hundreds of people swamped their stores trying to buy cheap stuff. They had to call the police and everything.'

Jack stared at the screen. 'Who knows what this Hector kid has planned for the virus then.' He reached over, clicked on the blinking red dot and brought up a street view of the road. The signal was coming from an apartment block. 'Look at the door.'

The front door was made of reinforced glass.

'That's got a Deadsight Three-Twelve lock.' Charlie leant over Obi's chair and spun the view left and right. The road was packed full of people. It was a busy part of London. 'There's no way to pick the lock without being spotted.' She straightened up and looked at Jack. 'Which means we'll need to use the gun.'

Jack stepped back, thinking. 'Yep.'

'So,' Charlie said. 'What's the plan? If we're using the gun, we'll need a distraction. Can't risk someone seeing it.'

Jack thought about it for a moment. 'We have to go *now*,' he said. 'That leaves us with only one solution.'

'Oh, wait a minute.' Slink's face lit up in realisation. 'Are you – are you saying . . .'

Jack nodded.

'*Yes.*' Slink punched the air. 'This month has been amazing. So much fun. And now we get to do The Phoenix?' He skipped in a circle like an excited four-year-old. 'I freakin love The Phoenix.'

Wren frowned at him. 'What's The Phoenix?'

'It's something we use whenever we don't have time to organise a proper mission,' Jack said. 'It's a form of distraction.'

'It's a last resort,' Charlie corrected.

Wren looked at Jack. 'Can I come with you?'

'Of course,' he said. 'You're going to be a key part of this.' His gaze moved to the clock on the main display. 'Be ready to go in ten minutes.'

Slink ran down the corridor to his room and shouted, 'This is going to be epic.'

'We need equipment.' Charlie gestured for Wren to follow her to the workshop.

Jack said to Obi, 'Run a check on this Hector kid. Find out everything you can.'

'Sure. Hey, Jack, you remember the last two times we tried The Phoenix, don't you?'

'Yep.'

Obi frowned. 'But, it didn't work, *either* time. Took us weeks to clean up the mess it caused.'

Jack strode towards his room. 'Third time's a charm,' he muttered. At least he hoped it would be.

• • •

In under an hour, Jack, Charlie and Wren were standing across the road from the kid's apartment.

Jack scoped out the area. There were six buildings, three each side of the road, facing one another. Their target was the red-brick one in the middle on the other side of the road. Facing it, on their side, was a white Georgian-style building.

Charlie jogged up the pavement, stopped outside the white apartment, glanced around to make sure she wasn't being watched, then bent down by the wall, as if doing up her shoelaces.

After a moment, she sprang to her feet and hurried back to Jack and Wren.

Jack stared at the red-brick building. No one was going in or out. *The Phoenix* was their best chance. Otherwise, they might be waiting all day.

A couple of minutes later, a kid strode up to them. He was skinny, like Slink, and wore a hoodie.

'Hey, Jack.'

'Hi. How are you?'

The kid sniffed and glanced around. 'Not so bad.' He looked at Charlie. 'All right?'

She nodded.

'Wren,' Jack said. 'This is Raze.'

Raze held his hand out. 'Nice to meet ya.'

Wren shook it. 'You too.' She let go and gave Jack a puzzled look.

'Raze is an explosives expert,' Jack said in a hushed voice. 'We use his skills from time to time.'

Raze slipped off his backpack and pulled out a rectangular object, the size of a shoebox, wrapped in brown paper.

Jack took it from him. 'Thanks.'

Raze fished in his pocket and handed Charlie a remote key fob. It had a small antenna and a large red button. 'Be careful with that,' he said. 'The trigger is sensitive.'

'OK.'

Raze gave her a crooked smile, then pulled his hood up and jogged away.

Jack looked at Wren. 'Right, see that white building with the pillars?'

Wren nodded.

'Charlie has drawn a cross on the pavement in blue chalk.'

'By the wall,' Charlie said.

'Exactly,' Jack said. 'By the wall. Take this.' He handed Wren the box. 'Put it exactly on the cross, take two big steps back, then scream as loud as you can and look up. Understand?'

Wren nodded.

'Good.' Jack glanced around. 'Go.' He squatted with Charlie between the bumpers of two parked cars.

Charlie pulled a paintball sniper rifle from her bag, screwed in the barrel and hopper, and handed it to him. 'Are you sure you don't want *me* to do this?'

'Nope.' Jack rested his arm on one of the bumpers and looked through the scope. 'This is all me.'

'You're *really* sure?'

Jack looked at her. 'What are you saying?'

Charlie hesitated. 'Well, Jack, the last two times –'

'I've got this, all right?'

Charlie held up her hands. 'Fine. Whatever. Just saying.' She looked at the red-brick building. 'But, you know, if you –'

'*Shut up.*'

'OK, OK. God.'

Jack watched Wren as she walked to the front wall of the white building and placed the box on the ground.

She took two steps back and screamed.

Wren then looked up and her eyes went wide.

She screamed again. This time it was louder and sounded a lot more authentic, like real shock.

Jack chuckled to himself – they'd not told Wren what was about to happen.

'I still think we should've warned her,' Charlie said.

'Nah, that second scream was much more believable.'

High above Wren's head, holding on to a window ledge by nothing more than the tips of his fingers, was Slink. He had his hood up, hiding his face, and he swung his legs from side to side as if trying to find something to grip on to. 'Help,' he cried. 'Please, please help me.'

A middle-aged woman rushed over to Wren and said something to her. Wren pointed up and the woman's gaze locked on Slink.

The woman cupped a hand over her mouth.

Jack focused on the glass front door of the red-brick building opposite. No one was coming out yet. 'Come on,' he muttered.

More people gathered around Wren. Jack watched the surprise and horror register on their faces as they spotted Slink above them. Some gasped while others shouted for help. Yet others pressed mobile phones to their ears, no doubt calling the emergency services. A few people held their phones up, taking pictures.

Slink continued to swing his legs back and forth as if he were panicking.

As the minutes passed, even more people gathered and the commotion increased.

Cars were stopping now.

Jack looked through the scope on the paintball sniper rifle. 'Bingo.'

A man and woman in their twenties came out of the red-brick building.

Jack kept his focus on the glass door as it started to close. He moved the cross hairs over the frame, down to the lock and squeezed the trigger.

There was a blast of air. A paintball flew from the barrel, across the road, and missed the lock, splattering the wall inside the foyer.

The door closed and the couple hurried over to the crowd of people, unaware of what had just happened.

Jack swore and glanced at Charlie. 'Don't say it.'

'I wasn't going to. Wait,' her eyes widened. '*Jack*.'

Jack looked through the scope as an old lady walked into the foyer of the red-brick building and peered through the glass at the crowd.

'Come outside,' Jack muttered. 'You can't see properly from there. Come out. You know you want to.'

The woman stood in the foyer for a full minute before she finally checked she had her keys on her and opened the door.

'That's right,' Jack breathed.

As soon as she stepped across the threshold, he took aim on the door lock, held his breath and squeezed the trigger.

The modified paintball hit the lock dead on and exploded, covering it in a thick glutinous substance. The door went to close but because of the glue, it held open.

Charlie's homemade paintball recipe had worked.

Jack handed her the gun and said into his microphone, 'Wren, time for you to get back here.'

Charlie folded the gun and slipped it into her bag.

Wren squeezed through the crowd of onlookers and ran over to them. 'Slink,' she said, her voice shrill. 'He's –'

'He's fine.' Charlie glared at Jack. 'Slink knows what he's doing.'

A fire engine pulled up to the kerb and several men jumped out.

'Time to get him out of there,' Jack said.

Charlie slipped the remote key fob from her pocket, took a breath and pressed the button.

There was a loud *pop* as the box Wren had placed by the wall exploded. The crowd of onlookers jumped back and some of them instinctively ducked. But, instead of flying shrapnel or flame, a huge ball of smoke erupted skyward.

In a couple of seconds, it enveloped Slink and continued to rise up the front of the white building.

When the smoke cleared, Slink was gone.

Wren stared, dumbfounded.

'Come on,' Charlie said, and they sprinted across the road and slipped into the red-brick building's foyer.

Jack pressed a finger to his ear. 'Have you got an apartment number, Obi?'

'Third floor. Flat twelve.'

They headed to the stairs and as they climbed them, Charlie said to Jack, 'I can't believe that actually worked this time.'

• • •

Jack, Charlie and Wren stood outside the door to apartment twelve.

'Keep an eye out,' Jack whispered. He slipped his backpack off, unzipped it and pulled out a flat camera mounted on a metal plate. A wire connected the camera to a portable LCD display, which he held in his other hand.

Jack quietly slid the camera under the door and an image of the hallway on the other side appeared on the monitor.

'Empty,' he whispered. 'No one in there.'

Charlie motioned for Wren to keep guard, while she set to work on the lock with her picks.

After a minute, the lock clicked and she stepped back.

Jack slid the camera from under the door and returned it to his bag. He stood up, grabbed the door handle and silently stepped inside, with Charlie and Wren close behind.

Charlie closed the door and they waited in the hallway, listening. The sound of a TV was coming from an open door to their right.

Jack glanced back at the others, put a finger to his lips and crept up to it, his back close to the wall.

He took a deep breath, then peered around the doorframe.

The room beyond was a teenager's bedroom. There was a single bed with black bed sheets. Posters hung on the wall – pictures of galaxies and space rockets. A TV sat on a dresser. A film was on. Jack recognised it as *War of the Worlds*. Alien spaceships were shooting laser weapons on a town, as people tried to run away.

Against the wall was a desk. Under it was a computer with its lights blinking. On the desk was also a laptop and next to that were thirty or forty origami shapes made out of chewing gum wrappers. Jack frowned at them – there were various birds and animals. One of them even looked like a –

There was a noise and Jack's head snapped to the left. Opposite the bedroom was a lounge and he caught sight of a kid pulling back a set of curtains and opening the window.

Jack ran into the room.

The kid started to climb out of the window, but he yelled and fell back.

Slink was outside, hanging upside down like a vampire bat. He grinned. 'Hello, mate.'

• • •

A minute later, the kid was sitting in an armchair, breathing heavily, sweat glistening on his forehead. He looked up at the four of them. 'What do you want?'

Jack folded his arms. 'So you're Hector.'

He hesitated. 'How do you know my name?'

'Where's the virus?'

Hector looked uneasily between them all before saying to Jack, 'Who are you?'

'Achilles.'

Hector's eyes went wide. 'Achilles? Serious? *The* Achilles who hacked the USKR bank?'

Jack glanced at Charlie. 'Maybe.'

'That means . . .' Hector looked between them all. 'Are you the Urban Outlaws?'

'How do you know that?' Wren said, aghast.

'You're kinda famous.'

'No we're not,' Jack said.

'Yes you are. Everyone on the Cerberus forum knows about you.' Hector had a look of awe on his face. 'You blew up that quantum computer, didn't you?'

'Proteus,' Slink said, lifting his chin.

Jack scowled at him, then his narrowed eyes locked on Hector again. 'Where's the virus?'

'What virus?'

Slink stepped forward. 'Want me to hang this bozo out of the window, Jack?'

Hector didn't flinch. 'I'm not scared of heights.'

'Oh, yeah?' Slink took another step forward. 'Guess you just ain't been high enough yet.'

Jack held up a hand.

Slink scowled at Hector and stepped back again.

Jack glanced around the apartment. 'Where are your parents?'

'Dad's away,' Hector said. 'Won't be back until next week. Mum's dead.'

'We know what you did. We know you broke into Bransgore power station.'

Hector's eyebrows rose. 'I didn't break in. There was already a hole in the fence.' He looked at Charlie and for the first time, a slight grin twitched his lips. Hector's eyes then moved to Slink and Wren. 'I watched what you two did to that guard. That was some impressive stuff.'

Slink nodded. 'Yeah, I know.'

'Thank you,' Wren said, beaming at Hector.

'That's not the point,' Jack said. 'We know you've got the virus. You have no idea how powerful it is.'

'Yes, I do,' Hector said. 'Why do you think I wanted it?'

Jack was caught off guard by this statement. He took a moment to compose himself before asking, 'How did you find out about it?'

'The blackouts, of course.'

'What about them?'

'Well, I knew something had to be moving from power station to power station. It was obvious.'

'Oh, really?'

Hector shrugged. 'Yeah. I figured it was probably

a virus moving through their systems.' He glanced round to the others again. 'As I said – it was obvious.'

Slink smiled and nudged Jack's arm. 'Obvious.'

Jack remained tight-lipped. 'You worked out it was a virus, so what then?'

Hector shuffled in his chair. 'I hacked into their systems and found it.' His eyes glazed over and he stared at the wall. 'It was amazing.'

'I know,' Jack said. 'Get to the point.'

'So,' Hector said, seeming to snap out of his trance. 'Knowing what the virus was capable of, I had to have it. I wanted to understand how it worked.'

Jack sighed. He'd wanted the same thing – to see how the virus ticked, but they had to grab it first, before it got even more out of control. 'What did you do next?'

'I was trying to work out a way to remove it when the techies cut the line to the internet. I knew I had to go and break in, try to remove it directly, but you lot beat me to it.'

Jack's eyes wandered to the bedroom across the hall. The laptop on the desk had his USB stick in the side port.

Charlie had spotted it too. She marched off to the bedroom and returned with them. She handed the stick to Jack.

'Is the virus on here?' he said.

Hector shook his head.

Jack frowned. 'Where is it then?'

Hector squeezed his eyes shut. 'Gone.'

'*What*?'

'Oh, that's flipping brilliant,' Slink shouted.

Hector opened his eyes. 'It slipped through my firewalls.'

'Of course it did, you idiot. That's what it does.'

'*Slink*,' Charlie hissed.

'What?' Slink threw his hands up and walked to the window.

'I know where the virus went though,' Hector said in a low voice. 'And I've been working on a plan to get it back.'

'Where is it?' Jack said.

'Look.' Hector leant forward in the chair. 'Let me join your gang.'

'No way.'

'I can help you,' Hector said, looking around at all of them. 'We can catch the virus together. I'd make a good Urban Outlaw. Come on, please?'

Jack opened his mouth to answer, but his earpiece crackled.

'Guys?' It was Obi, and it sounded as though it was urgent.

Jack turned away and pressed a finger to his ear. 'Can't it wait? We're just about to find out where the virus has gone.'

'You might want to look out of the window.'

Jack hurried over and peered down. 'Oh.' A black SUV pulled up at the kerb. 'No way.'

'What's wrong?' Charlie joined him and when she saw what he was looking at, she gasped. 'How the –'

Benito Del Sarto's henchman – Connor – climbed out of the driver's side.

Charlie said, 'Why isn't he in prison?'

Connor had tried to kill the Outlaws on several occasions.

The nightmare got worse – Monday, a man so big that he looked like he could pick up a sumo wrestler in each hand and not break into a sweat, stepped out of the back of the SUV. Last, Cloud, a smartly dressed woman got out the of front-passenger side.

'This is not happening.' Jack spun around. 'We've got to get out of here.'

'What's going on?' Hector said.

'Bad people,' Charlie said. '*Very* bad people.'

'What do they want?'

'I'll give you one guess.' Jack stepped in front of him. 'Last chance – where's the virus?'

Hector looked at the window. 'I'm not telling you.'

'What?' Jack said, incredulous. 'Yes, you are.'

Hector's eyes moved to him. 'You say those people are here for the virus?'

Jack nodded.

'Then you've got to take me with you.'

'We're not recruiting,' Jack said. 'Tell us where it is or –'

'Or what?' Hector said.

They glared at each other.

Slink peered out of the window. 'We haven't got time for this.'

'I'll make a pact,' Hector said in a calm voice. 'Take me with you and I'll tell you where the virus has gone.'

Jack shook his head. 'No deal.'

'Jack.' Charlie grabbed his arm. 'We can't leave him for Connor to find.'

'Yeah,' Slink said. 'They might beat the virus's location out of him.'

Jack's eyes didn't move from Hector's. 'Where. Is. It?'

Hector sat back in his chair and crossed his arms.

'They'll be here any moment,' Slink said, his voice urgent. 'Are we staying to fight them?'

'No, we're not,' Charlie said. 'Please, Jack, let's go.'

Jack hesitated, then he said to Hector through a clenched jaw, 'OK. You're coming with us, but if you try to run, we'll –'

'I won't run.' Hector stood up, grabbed a backpack from a table and held his hand out to Charlie. 'Laptop, please.'

She handed it to him and there was a knock at the front door.

CHAPTER SEVEN

JACK, CHARLIE, SLINK AND WREN SPRINTED down the hallway, following Hector into a cramped kitchen. He pulled up a blind, opened the window and scrambled out on to the fire escape.

Jack motioned for Wren to go next.

She climbed up and Hector helped her through.

There was another knock, louder this time.

'Go,' Jack said to Slink.

Slink jumped through the open window in one fluid movement.

Jack gestured for Charlie to hurry up too.

There was a loud bang as a heavy object rammed into the front door. Jack glanced down the hallway. He could guess what that object was – Monday's shoulder or foot.

Charlie ducked through the window frame.

There was another bang, a cracking sound, and

the front door burst open, the wood shattering and sending splinters flying.

Monday stepped into the hallway and dusted himself off.

Connor followed and, for a second, his cold eyes met with Jack's. Connor's face twisted into rage.

Jack leapt through the window and raced after the others. He clattered down the metal steps, almost tripping. 'Hurry up,' he urged.

Halfway to the bottom, Jack glanced up to see Connor staring down at him.

Connor reached under his jacket.

Jack turned and vaulted the remaining steps. He'd learnt from experience that Connor would not hesitate to shoot a bunch of kids. '*Run.*'

They sprinted along the alleyway, around the building, and skidded to a halt.

Cloud stood in front of them, blocking their escape. She had her right hand under her jacket. 'Don't move.'

For a few seconds, no one did, then Hector spun on his heels and sprinted back around the corner.

There was no time to think. Jack, Charlie, Slink and Wren followed him, with Cloud in pursuit.

Connor and Monday were still hurrying down the metal fire escape.

As the Outlaws ran past, Connor cleared the steps and lunged for them. Wren ducked under his outstretched arms.

Connor roared his annoyance.

Hector reached the end of the alleyway and sprinted right. 'Come on,' he shouted.

They raced after him and dashed across a main road.

Tyres screeched and horns sounded.

Slink vaulted over the bonnet of a black cab.

The driver wound down his window, swore and waved his fist at them.

On the other side of the road, Hector darted left. 'Follow me.' He sprinted across the street and down another alleyway. At the end, they went right, followed the back of the buildings and came out at a small park.

They stopped, catching their breath, sure they were out of sight and hadn't been followed.

'What now?' Charlie said, panting and glancing around.

Jack looked at Hector. 'It's time you told us where the virus has gone.'

Hector hesitated.

Jack's eyes narrowed. 'Tell us. *Now.*'

'Nexus,' Hector said. 'OK? It went to somewhere called Nexus.'

'What's that?'

Hector shrugged. 'I don't know exactly. I got a glimpse of that name in a line of code. I think it's some sort of government project.'

Jack looked at Charlie. 'We've wasted our time.'

'No,' Hector said. 'I can find out where the virus went. My trace program was running automatically when it moved from my laptop. With a bit of work, I can get a location for this Nexus thing.'

Jack couldn't help but show a huge amount of doubt in his expression.

'Let him try,' Charlie said. 'We don't have any other leads.'

Jack thought for a moment. What he wanted to do was get rid of Hector, send him home, but he knew too much. If Jack let Hector go now, he could reveal the existence of the virus to other people. As it stood, the Outlaws had a head start on anyone else that might be hunting it. Especially Connor.

So, that gave Jack little choice.

He sighed. 'Fine. You can stay.'

For now, anyway, Jack thought.

Hector nodded and Wren smiled at him.

'So,' Charlie said. 'What's next?'

'Noble,' Jack said. 'If anyone knows what this Nexus is, it's him. Come on.'

'Who's Noble?' Hector asked, but Jack didn't respond.

As they walked through the park, Charlie slid a phone from her pocket and keyed a quick message. A few minutes passed and no one answered. 'Where is he?' They reached the main gate. 'Wait,' she said. 'What day is it?'

'Thursday,' Slink said.

'No,' Wren said. 'It's Tuesday.'

'Yeah, Tuesday,' Jack agreed.

'That's why I can't get hold of him.' Charlie looked at Jack. 'He's at the Science Museum.'

'I remember,' Jack said. Noble had told them there was a special exhibition on Alan Turing that he wanted to see.

'Why doesn't he just put his phone on vibrate?' Hector said.

'He doesn't have a phone,' Charlie said. 'When I send him messages, it's always through email.'

Hector frowned. 'That's just stupid.'

'Noble is *not* stupid,' Jack said, annoyed. 'He's a genius.'

Hector's eyebrows rose. 'Then why doesn't he have a phone?'

'A few reasons. The main one is that he doesn't trust them. Thinks they're too easily traced.'

'He's right,' Charlie said. 'They are a lot of hassle. We have to keep changing phones and SIM cards all the time.'

Hector looked at Jack again. 'Can we wait for him?'

Jack shook his head. 'He's likely to be in there all day. We'll have to go get him.' He glanced around. 'Where's the nearest Tube station?'

Hector pointed towards an Underground sign on the other side of the park.

They all pulled their hoods up and marched towards it.

When they reached the top of the steps, Slink glanced back. 'Er, guys.'

Connor, Cloud and Monday were running towards them.

'Go,' Jack shouted, and they hurried down into the Underground.

People protested as they shoved past them. At

the bottom of the stairs, they ran right, then left towards the ticket barriers.

Hector stopped short. 'We need tickets.'

'No we don't,' Charlie said, pulling several Oyster cards from her pocket. Each one gave them unlimited credit to travel on the Tube.

Charlie handed Jack, Slink and Wren a card each. She then swiped hers over the reader, the barrier opened and she stepped through.

Wren and Slink did the same.

Jack glanced back to see Connor, Monday and Cloud pushing through the throng of people.

He chucked his card at Hector. 'Hurry.'

Monday spotted Jack and pointed.

The three of them continued to shove their way past the crowd.

Hector swiped the card over the reader and stepped through the barrier. He turned back and tossed it to Jack.

The card slipped through Jack's fingers and hit the floor. Cursing, he bent down and scooped it up.

Connor lunged forward as Jack swiped the card and slipped through just in time.

He stood on the other side of the barrier, staring back at a snarling Connor.

In desperation and anger, Connor started to climb over the barrier.

'Oi, what's your game?' A Tube attendant shouted.

Connor kept his eyes on Jack.

The Tube attendant grabbed him and pulled him back.

'Get your hands off me.'

Jack wheeled around and hurried to the others. 'This way.' They jogged to a set of escalators that led down. At the bottom, he said, 'Left-hand platform.'

Charlie hesitated. 'But Noble is –'

'*Left*,' Jack insisted. They ran along the platform to the end and tried to blend in with the commuters.

Jack kept glancing at the stairs. The seconds stretched into minutes.

After what seemed an eternity, he heard the unmistakable low rumble of an approaching train and warm air brushed past his face.

Connor, Monday and Cloud stepped on to the platform just as the train pulled in.

The doors opened and the five of them jumped on board.

It was too late – Connor, Cloud and Monday had spotted them and also climbed on, a few carriages back.

'Jack,' Charlie hissed.

'I know.' Jack looked at the doors. 'On three.' He glanced at the others and they nodded. 'One.' Jack saw Connor, Cloud and Monday making their way through the carriages towards them. 'Two.' The door to the next carriage opened and Del Sarto's operatives stepped inside. The main doors beeped and started to close. *Three.*

Jack and the others leapt from the train just as the doors closed behind them.

The train pulled away from the platform and Slink waved as an enraged Connor stared through the carriage windows as they shot past.

Chuckling to themselves, the Outlaws strode to the other platform and stepped on to another train going in the opposite direction.

• • •

Twenty minutes later, Jack, Charlie, Slink, Wren and Hector were standing in front of the Science Museum in South Kensington.

Jack turned to Hector. 'Wait here.'

'Why can't he come with us?' Wren said.

'It's OK,' Hector said, before Jack could answer. 'I understand.' He smiled at the others, but the grin slipped from his face when he looked at Jack again.

'Stay here with him,' Jack said to Slink.

Until they knew exactly what this Nexus was and what they were dealing with, Jack didn't want Hector out of their sight.

Wren scowled at Jack, but he turned his back on her.

As they walked into the museum, Jack heard her mutter something to Charlie about him being paranoid and rude. Jack couldn't understand how reckless the others were being when it came to Hector.

They tried to look as casual as possible and Jack put some money in the donations box as they passed into the main hall.

The whole place was buzzing with kids and parents.

'This way,' Jack said.

They hurried to a flight of stairs and at the top was the exhibition on Alan Turing – one of the early pioneers of computer technology and code breaking. There was a huge black-and-white photo of him. As they turned the corner, on the right-hand side, behind a large sheet of glass, was a wooden cabinet with dials and switches.

Noble stood staring at it. He was a tall, slender man, with dark skin and silver hair tied back in a ponytail. He wore a long coat and had a peaceful expression on his face.

Jack, Charlie and Wren gathered around him.

'What is that?' Wren said, frowning at the wooden cabinet.

'Pilot ACE,' Jack said. 'It was one of the fastest computers in the nineteen-fifties.'

'That's right.' Noble turned and his eyebrows rose. 'What are you three doing here?'

'We need your help,' Jack said.

Noble glanced around to make sure no one was listening in on their conversation. 'Explain.'

Jack quickly brought Noble up to speed about the virus, how trying to capture it had led them to Hector, then Connor and his sidekicks had turned up but the Outlaws had managed to get away.

Noble listened patiently and finally said, 'I gather you want to get to the virus before Del Sarto's people or the secret service do?'

Jack nodded and, keeping his voice low, said, 'Hector thinks he knows where the virus has gone.'

'Where?'

'Have you heard of something called the Nexus?'

Noble looked taken aback. 'I should hope so,' he said. 'I helped create it.'

Now it was Jack who had an astonished look on his face. 'You did?'

A group of tourists walked past.

Noble gestured for Jack, Charlie and Wren to follow him. As they walked, he spoke in barely a whisper. 'Five years ago, I was asked to help on a secret project. At the time, I wasn't informed of what it was. At first, I assumed the Nexus was some kind of advanced game.' He looked at Jack. 'It has high-end programming like no one has ever seen before. They used the best people in the world.' Noble stopped in front of a display cabinet that held yet another old-fashioned computer. It had wires and buttons jutting out from every angle. He stared at it as he spoke. 'Six months before the project was due to be completed, I was asked to leave.'

'Why?' Jack said.

'I think they didn't want me to see what the Nexus was going to be used for.'

'But you know?'

Noble walked between the display cabinets again. 'The Nexus is a state-of-the-art, three-dimensional virtual world, created by the British Ministry of Defence.'

'For what?' Charlie said.

'They use it for multiple purposes.' Noble stopped in front of a cabinet with another old computer inside. 'The Nexus is a secret meeting facility. A place where their field agents can report in without having to compromise their locations.' He lowered his voice even further. 'The SAS also use it as an advanced training program – a way to rehearse for missions.' Noble's gaze roamed for a second. 'I also heard that the Ministry of Defence run simulations of terrorist attacks.'

'What's the hardware like?' Charlie said.

Noble waited until a family went past them and he whispered, 'Out of this world. Hundreds of processors dedicated just to graphics.'

'So,' Charlie said. 'The virus was attracted to the Nexus somehow? Because of its power?'

Noble considered this for a moment. 'It's probably one of the most powerful facilities in the United Kingdom. However, I wouldn't have thought it would go there of its own accord.'

'I don't think so either,' Jack said. 'They must have sent a signal to attract it.' The same technique he'd tried by using his program on the USB stick.

'Yes,' Noble said. 'Which means they understand the virus's potential to be developed into the world's best hacking tool.' He walked a few more paces and stopped next to another display cabinet with some kind of antique keyboard under a CRT monitor. 'The virus is able to slip past any security system – quite a power if it can be harnessed or even worked out and duplicated.'

'Exactly,' Jack said. 'That's why they want the virus – to learn from it. They'll dissect it and manipulate it to work for them.' The thought made him feel sick. It was Proteus all over again.

'Why put it in a virtual world though?' Charlie said. 'I don't get it.'

'Well, you did destroy their most advanced computer.' Noble winked at them. 'The Nexus is the only thing the government have left that's powerful enough to hold the virus.'

'But it still doesn't make sense,' Charlie said slowly. 'Why would they put the virus in the Nexus? It could damage it.' She glanced at Jack. 'It's already taken down one of their secret facilities, a whole load of power stations, a supercomputer and God knows what else. Why would they risk it?'

'Like Noble says,' Jack replied, 'high risk means

high reward. They know the virus could be turned into the world's best hacker.'

'I think they'd also have it under control. For now, anyway,' Noble said. 'The virus didn't completely cripple Proteus, just stopped it from working properly. The Nexus is no slouch either – it makes a games console look like a plastic tiddlywinks set. It has vast arrays of hard drives and processors. It would take a long while for the virus to affect it all.' He shrugged. 'Besides, if it gets too much, they'll simply shut it down and work out how to either resolve the problem or remove the virus entirely.' He looked at Jack again. 'Was it still mutating when you last saw it?'

Jack nodded. 'Yeah.'

Noble stared off into the distance.

'What?' Charlie said. 'What are you thinking?'

Noble glanced around again and they continued walking slowly between the exhibition displays, keeping their distance from the other visitors.

Finally, he said, 'The Nexus is a good place for them to observe the virus. The code will be too complex to understand in its raw form, too quick to change. I believe they're using the Nexus as not only a place to trap the virus, but also as a way to visualise it in three-dimensions. A way to understand how it works.'

'How do we get inside this Nexus thing?' Wren asked.

'Ah,' Noble said. 'Now that's the question, isn't it? It's not usually connected to the internet. They must have only opened the doors to the Nexus just that one time. And now they've sealed it off again, the virus will have no way out.'

'And we'll have no way in,' Charlie said.

'Yes.'

'Brilliant. So it's gone?'

Jack let out a snort of annoyance. No matter what they did, they just kept meeting new problems. 'Wait a minute,' he said. 'The virus went from Hector's laptop to the Nexus, and he said he can trace the location.'

Noble's eyes widened. 'An access point?'

'A what?'

'The Nexus is on its own secure system. As I said, they must have connected it to the internet briefly to trap the virus, but they would've used an access point. An access point is a direct connection to the Nexus. A way to interface with it without actually going to where the Nexus is physically located.'

'Where is the Nexus?' Wren said.

'I don't know.'

'But we can connect to it via an access point?' Charlie said.

'Yes. There are a few scattered around the country, but I've never heard of their locations either.' Noble looked thoughtful for a moment. 'If you can find an access point, there's a good chance you can log on to the Nexus.'

A flood of hope washed over Jack. 'So, there's a way?'

Noble nodded. 'If your friend can provide us with the location, I can help you with the rest.' A sly grin cracked his lips.

They all smiled back at him.

• • •

Outside, they met up with Hector and Slink, and walked back to the main road.

A way down, Noble stopped outside an alleyway. 'I've parked there,' he said, pointing at a ramp that led to a garage under a building. 'They have security. I suggest you all wait here.' He strode across the road.

Jack, Charlie, Slink, Wren and Hector pulled back into the shadows and waited.

Jack pressed a finger to his ear. 'Obi?'

'Yeah?'

'Did you hear all that?'

'Everything,' Obi said. 'And I've been searching for any references to this Nexus place on the Cerberus forum.'

'And?'

'Nothing.'

Jack watched cars go past. 'Well, Noble says it definitely exists.'

'Let's hope Hector can find it then,' Obi said.

Jack lowered his voice to barely a whisper. 'While we're on that, Obi, have you found anything on Hector's background?'

'Looks clean, so far.'

'OK, keep digging and let me know if –'

'Get off me!'

Jack spun around.

Connor was grasping Slink's throat. 'One false move and I'll break his neck.'

CHAPTER EIGHT

JACK STOOD IN STUNNED SILENCE, WATCHING Connor squeeze Slink's throat.

Slink was starting to turn blue and, for the first time in his life, Jack couldn't think of a way to help him.

'Keep still,' Connor growled in Slink's ear, 'and you might live through this.'

'Get off him.' Wren went to step forward, but Jack grabbed her arm. He looked around the alleyway, but still couldn't see a way to save Slink.

'Stand in front of me,' Hector whispered to Charlie. 'Block his view.' He slipped the backpack off his shoulders.

'What are you doing?' Jack hissed through the corner of his mouth.

'Keep him distracted.'

Connor said something and Jack looked at him.

'We haven't got the virus,' Charlie said, defiant.

Connor's eyes were mere slits. 'Of course you have. Give it to me.'

Slink tried to twist his body free.

'Careful, boy,' Connor snarled and dug his fingers in. He looked at Jack. 'The virus.'

'We've told you – we don't have it.'

'I'm not falling for your tricks again,' Connor said, redoubling his grip on Slink's neck and making him grimace. With his free hand, Connor reached into his pocket and pulled out a phone.

Obviously, he was calling Monday and Cloud for backup.

'Leave this to me,' Hector whispered.

Jack glanced at him and then did a double take.

Hector was wearing some kind of gauntlet. It was black and had plastic cylinders moulded to the back of it. Cables ran from the cylinders and down the fingers, ending in silver pads on the tips.

'What are you doing?' Jack mumbled. 'What is that?'

Suddenly, Hector burst forward, springing past Jack, Charlie and Wren and leaping towards Connor.

Connor started to react, but he was too slow – Hector rammed into him, knocking him backwards.

Just as Slink twisted free, Hector reached out and touched Connor's arm with the gloved hand.

There was a loud *crack* and Connor crumpled to the floor.

Hector spun around. '*Run*,' he shouted.

They sprinted down the alleyway just as Noble's blue campervan pulled to the kerb.

Jack slid open the side door and they all clambered in.

'Go,' Jack shouted.

Noble stamped his foot on the accelerator and pulled away.

Half a mile down the road, he said, 'What just happened?'

'Connor,' Jack said, pulling back the curtains and checking the cars behind them. Satisfied no one was following, he sat down and allowed himself to relax.

'I owe you one, mate,' Slink said to Hector.

Hector waved him off. 'Don't worry about it.'

'You were amazing,' Wren said.

Jack winced inside. He felt bad that it hadn't been him who'd got Slink out of that mess.

Charlie nodded at Hector's gauntlet. 'Is that a stun glove?'

'Yes. It delivers three-hundred thousand volts.'
Hector slipped it off and stuffed it back into his bag.

'Did you build it?'

'Yeah.'

'Impressive.'

Jack let out a slow breath and looked around.

The interior of Noble's campervan was kitted out with a leather chair surrounded by monitors and computers. Noble called the van his mobile command centre.

At the back was a bench where Jack, Charlie and Hector sat. Wren and Slink sat cross-legged on the floor.

Noble parked, climbed out of the driver's seat and dropped into the chair.

Jack turned to Hector. 'So you reckon you can find where the Nexus is?'

'An access point,' Charlie corrected.

'Right,' Jack said. 'Access point.' He looked at Hector again. 'Can you find it or not?'

Hector nodded. 'No problem.'

'Do it.'

Hector pulled the laptop out of his bag, opened it, and started typing and clicking.

Jack watched over his shoulder as he worked.

'I know a quicker way of doing that,' he said. 'If you route through the –'

'You're wrong,' Hector said. 'This cuts out the need for extra proxies and spoofing my MAC address.' He brought up a dialog box. 'Watch this, you might learn something.'

Jack sat back and crossed his arms.

A minute later, Hector said, 'OK, they've left a direct trail. Doesn't even look like they tried to hide their footprints.' He looked at Jack with a smug expression. 'I've got the location.'

Noble pulled a keyboard towards him and Hector relayed the GPS coordinates. Noble then angled a monitor so the rest of them could see.

'According to Hector's information, the Nexus access point is located in a bookshop on Marylebone High Street.'

'A bookshop?' Jack said, incredulous. 'That can't be right.'

'Why not?' Hector said. 'Could be hidden under it.'

'I tend to agree.' Noble looked thoughtful. 'It's a good place to hide an access point – somewhere semi-public.' He looked at Hector. 'Quite clever, really. Well done on finding it. That can't have been easy.'

Hector smiled at him. 'Thanks.'

Jack clenched his fists. 'Any ideas on how to break in?' he asked.

'You'll have to figure that out for yourselves,' Noble said. 'Also, you will need a special piece of equipment to connect to the Nexus access point once you're inside.'

'What equipment?' Hector said. 'How do we get it?'

Jack glanced at him, annoyed. *What was with all this "We"?*

Noble cleared his throat. 'It just so happens, I acquired a set a while back.'

'Acquired?' Charlie said, aiming a wry grin in his direction.

Noble winked at her.

'OK,' Jack said. 'So, we break into the Nexus access point under the bookshop and find a way to extract the virus.'

As if it was going to be that easy.

Charlie looked at him. 'Sounds like this might be fun.'

• • •

Noble drove the five of them to London Docklands.

'Are we going to your house?' Wren asked Noble.

164

'Yes.'

'No, we're not,' Jack said. 'Drop him off here.' He glanced at Hector. 'We'll pick you up when we're done.'

'Jack,' Charlie said, frowning. 'Hector just saved Slink's life. Show him some respect.'

'Respect?' Jack said, incredulous. 'Are you kidding? You do remember he stole the virus from us?'

Charlie shot him a stern look.

'Whatever,' Jack muttered.

But they did have a problem – if they ditched Hector, he might try to break into the Nexus on his own, or worse, tell other people about what they were trying to do. Not to mention the fact that Connor could get hold of him.

Jack ground his teeth. Charlie was right – they had to keep Hector with them. They had no choice.

Besides, he thought, *there is a saying about keeping your enemies close.*

He glanced at the others. Why did they trust Hector so much? They'd been in worse situations and Jack had got them out before. He would've thought of a way to save Slink, if he'd just been given the chance.

Jack took a deep breath and tried to relax.

The time would come when the others would agree with him. They'd let Hector go and it would be just the five of them again. Back to normal.

Hector gazed out of the window, oblivious to Jack's burning stare. He was looking at the old and new buildings mixed together, lining the Thames. 'What are we doing here?'

Slink pointed through the windscreen at a huge Georgian brick warehouse.

They drove down a side road and headed to the rear of the building. On the back wall was an enormous faded poster of a painted image of Titanic, surrounded by a fancy rope border. Strangely enough, it advertised something called "toilet soap".

Noble turned the campervan and drove straight towards the sign.

Hector tensed visibly.

Wren smiled at him. 'Watch this,' she said.

When they were a few metres from the wall, the entire sign rose up into the air, revealing an archway beyond.

Noble drove through, parked the campervan inside the building and they all climbed out as the sign lowered back into place.

They were now standing in a room filled with antique cars, motorbikes and bicycles. There was an old boxy Ford car with wooden wheels, a two-seater Triumph, a silver Aston Martin and even a pink and white ice-cream van.

There were also around twenty or so motorbikes of various makes and ages lined up in a neat row. Only Charlie and Noble knew all of their names.

Around the edges of the room were fifty or so bicycles. One Jack did recognise was called a Raleigh Chopper. It had high, sweeping handlebars, a curved seat and a gear stick on the main crossbars.

Above all the bikes, metal signs filled every available wall space, advertising oil, petrol, even Hot Coffee.

The round pillars that held up the ceiling were covered in car badges and old tax discs.

Hector stared at the complete scene, dumbfounded. 'It's like a museum in here.'

'Noble,' Charlie said, hurrying over to a red Formula One car in the corner of the room by the ice-cream van. 'When did you get this?' She walked slowly around it, her eyes wide.

'A couple of months ago,' Noble said with half a smile.

'It's a two thousand and five, Team Ferrari, F1.'
Charlie looked up at him. 'How did you get it?'

Noble shrugged. 'An auction.'

'Must have cost you a fortune.'

Noble cleared his throat. 'It was an *online* auction.'

'Let me guess,' Jack said. 'By some miracle, you were the only one who bid on it because the other bidders mysteriously vanished?'

Noble shrugged. 'Something like that.'

'I want a Ferrari,' Wren said.

'That's more your speed.' Slink pointed at a bicycle with a ginormous front wheel.

'Penny-farthing.' Noble walked to the far wall, pulled up a wooden shutter and stepped into a lift. The others followed him inside. Charlie reluctantly tore her eyes from the Ferrari and hurried over to them. When she was in, Noble was about to pull down the shutter, but Jack stopped him.

He turned to Hector. 'Wait by the van.'

'*Jack*,' Charlie said. 'Are you serious?'

Slink and Wren frowned at him too.

Jack ignored them and pointed at a camera high on the wall. 'We'll be watching you.'

'It's OK,' Hector said to the others. 'I'm cool with it.' But the nasty look he gave Jack said otherwise.

Hector stepped out of the lift.

Noble pulled down the shutter and hit the button on the wall.

Jack felt the others staring at him, but he ignored them.

The entire first level of the warehouse was open-plan and divided into various living areas, each filled with a mixture of gadgets and antiques. The old and the new were stacked together, with barely space to walk between them.

Starting in the top left corner was Noble's living area with a sofa made out of a Volkswagen Beetle with the main cabin and roof removed. Above it was a huge crystal chandelier.

The right-hand side of the warehouse was divided into a kitchen and dining room like the Outlaws' bunker.

Back on the left side of the warehouse, next to Noble's lounge, was a work area with shelves crammed full of books, and in the middle was a metal desk with Noble's computer station. It was a lot neater than Obi's, with a PC case made from transparent acrylic, wireless keyboard and trackpad, and three high-resolution twenty-seven-inch screens, all next to a window that overlooked the River Thames.

The only other item on Noble's desk was a photo of Serene. Serene was Noble's sister. She lived in America, but came over from time to time to help with missions. She had a degree in chemistry, another in physics and one in business studies. She was clever. *Very* clever, and Jack missed her.

Noble hung his coat up on a stand made from old light fittings welded together and strode to his work area. Under the window were oak cupboards and drawers that matched the kitchen. Noble opened one cupboard, removed a metal briefcase and laid it on a table. 'Come and take a look at what I have here.'

They gathered around him as he undid the clasps and opened the case.

Jack leant forward and peered inside. Protected in black, cut-out foam was a set of video glasses, a pair of gloves covered in sensors and wires and a metal box with connections on the back. 'What's that?'

Noble pursed his lips. 'It's the equipment you need to connect to the Nexus.'

'They use some sort of virtual-reality gear for this?' Charlie said. 'Plug themselves in?' Her eyes glistened at the prospect of another gadget she could take apart and examine.

Noble nodded. 'As you can imagine, it was extremely hard to get this.'

Charlie's shoulders slumped as she realised she wouldn't be dismantling these.

'As far as I can tell,' Noble continued, 'they've only made a limited number of them.' He pointed at a number eight on a small brass plaque on the arm of the glasses.

'Guess we shouldn't break it then.' Slink reached in and hefted the glasses. 'Heavy.'

Noble eyed him. 'Care would be advisable.'

Jack took the glasses from Slink, lowered them back into the case and looked at Noble. 'Why do we need to use them?'

'It's the only way in,' Noble said. 'There are no other interfaces.'

Charlie looked confused. 'No keyboards, mice, displays?'

Noble shook his head. 'Nothing. Just the glasses and gloves.' His eyes moved to Jack. 'You'll have to go into the Nexus and look for the virus.'

'Then what?'

Noble shrugged. 'Find a way to extract it. As I said, I don't know what the final design looks like because my contract ended before the Nexus was

171

completed. You'll have to work it out when you get there.'

Jack pointed at the wires and connections. 'Think you could patch into that?' he said to Charlie.

She stared for a moment, then understood what he was getting at. 'Yeah. But why do you want to do that? What if the virus leaks to the internet again?'

'It won't,' Jack said. 'We'll use our phones to create a direct link with the bunker's computers.' He pressed a finger to his ear. 'Obi?'

'I heard,' Obi said. 'I have an idea.'

'What's that?'

'Outlaw World.'

'That's brilliant.' Jack glanced at Charlie – she was grinning. 'Obi, how long will it take you to set that up?'

'Not long. I have it all ready, just need to create a secure route via the phones.'

Jack closed the lid on the case, fastened the clasps and looked at Noble. 'Is there anything else we need to know?'

Noble considered this. 'I'm not sure what security you'll encounter, but the bookshop itself is in an old building.'

Jack smiled at Charlie, Slink and Wren. 'That's their first mistake.'

They beamed back at him.

• • •

Later that afternoon, Jack, Charlie, Hector, Slink and Wren sat at a table by the window in Vivaldi café, across the road from an old-fashioned bookshop with green wooden window frames and thick uneven glass. It was strangely fascinating and very few people could walk past the shop without taking a quick look inside.

The others explained to Hector why they were there, despite Jack's obvious unease about telling him too much.

'Here,' Charlie said to Hector. 'Wear this.' She pulled a headset from her bag and passed it to him. 'Say hi to Obi.'

Hector stuffed the earpiece in. 'Who's Obi?'

'*I'm* Obi.'

'He's back at the bunker,' Wren said.

'You live in a bunker?' Hector said. 'Where is it?'

'*Wren*,' Jack snapped.

Her brow furrowed. 'Why does it matter?'

'Because it does.' Jack didn't have time to explain.

'That's cool,' Hector muttered. 'I'd love to see it one day.'

Jack huffed. The others were being infuriating.

Slink leant over the table to Hector. 'You wanna know why he's called Obi?'

Hector nodded.

'It's short for Obi-Wan Kenobi,' Obi said. 'Obi-Wan was –'

'No it's not,' Slink interrupted. 'Obi's short for Oafish Blundering Idiot.'

Obi started swearing over Slink's laughs.

A waiter approached the table. He looked between them all and didn't seem very pleased that five kids were in the café unsupervised. 'What do you want?' he said in a haughty Italian accent.

'Five lemonades,' Slink said, grinning at him.

The waiter nodded and scribbled in his order pad. 'Anything to eat?'

'Just the lemonade.'

The waiter's eyes narrowed. He spun on his heels and marched away.

Jack refocused on the bookshop across the street.

A few minutes passed and the waiter returned

with a tray of drinks. He set the lemonades down and shuffled off.

Charlie said, 'While we wait, can we play the "Jack" game?'

Jack glanced at her. 'No.'

'Come on.'

'I said no.'

Hector looked puzzled. 'What's the "Jack" game?'

Slink said, 'Hi . . . Jack.'

Charlie suppressed a smile. 'Carjack.'

Jack shook his head. 'You know this is childish, right?'

'Lumberjack,' Obi said in his ear.

Everyone but Jack laughed.

Wren sat up straight and said, 'Flapjack.'

Jack looked at her. 'Not you too.'

'Ooh, ooh,' Obi said. 'Skyjack.'

Charlie said, 'Steeplejack.'

Still laughing, Slink said, 'Now the other way.' He cleared his throat dramatically. 'Jackdaw, jackknife, jackpot, jackhammer –'

'Enough,' Jack said. 'Game over.'

Slink scowled and muttered, 'Jacka–'

'*Slink*,' Charlie said, stifling a laugh.

Jack took a gulp of lemonade and stood up. He

fished in his pocket, pulled out some money and tossed it on to the table. He looked at Hector, Slink and Wren. 'You three wait here while Charlie and I go check out the bookshop.' Wren and Slink started to protest, but Jack held up a hand, silencing them. 'I need to see what we've got to work with, and if we get caught, we'll need you three to bail us out.'

Before the others could argue any further, Jack and Charlie hurried to the door, stepped outside, then jogged across the road and into the bookshop.

The interior was lined floor-to-ceiling with oak shelves. Jack and Charlie made their way to the back where the shop suddenly opened up in an impressive gallery with tall windows and skylights.

Jack glanced around. He thought Noble was right – the entrance to the Nexus access point wouldn't be up here.

'Come on,' he whispered, and they hurried down a flight of stairs.

The basement was also lined with oak bookshelves and there were no customers.

'Cameras,' Jack whispered, pulling up his hood and bandana, hiding his face.

Charlie did the same and the two of them moved

to the back wall. There was an emergency exit in the corner and no other rooms.

Charlie glanced around. 'You think it's behind one of these shelves?'

'Yeah.'

'But, how are we going to find it?'

'Ventilation,' Jack said.

Charlie frowned. 'Huh?'

'The room must be ventilated, right? There has to be a flow of air?'

'I guess so. Why?'

Jack slipped off his backpack and pulled out a small bag of chalk powder that they used for climbing.

He took a pinch of the powder and put it on to the palm of his right hand. He glanced around, then moved to a set of shelves. Jack gently blew across his palm, sending a puff of chalk into the air. The powder drifted to the floor.

Jack took several steps sideways and repeated the process.

There was still no discernible movement of air.

He moved to the shelves next to the exit and blew another puff of chalk into the air. The powder started to drop and then gently drifted towards the edge of the bookshelves.

'Got it,' he whispered to Charlie. 'It's behind this block of shelves.' He started touching the books, removed a couple and examined the wall behind them. 'There's got to be a trigger here somewhere.' His eyes scanned the walls and ceiling, then he walked back to the far end of the shelves where he'd seen the movement of powder. There was a gap between the shelf and the corner of the wall but he couldn't see a catch or handle of any kind.

'Wait a minute,' Charlie whispered. 'Keep an eye out.'

Jack glanced back – there were still no other customers down there.

Charlie rummaged inside her backpack and pulled out a device the same size as a mobile phone. It had three lights on the front – one red, one orange, one green, a small display, a dial and several switches on the side.

'What's that?' Jack whispered.

'It does a few things, but I can use it to find power cables inside walls.'

'Good thinking.'

Charlie moved to the shelf and waved the cable detector slowly along the books. The light on the device stayed green.

Finally, towards the top of the shelves, along the same side where Jack had found air movement, the cable detector's red LED came on. 'Wait a minute.' Charlie turned a dial on the detector. 'I'm setting this to transmit a radio pulse.' After a moment examining the display, she turned the dial again and then whispered, 'I thought so, there's a radio receiver on the other side of this shelf. They must use some kind of transmitter to open the door.'

'Coded?' Jack said.

'Yeah, but I think I can get it.' She held the device above her head for a moment, then examined the display. Charlie memorised the number, pulled a key fob from her pocket and pressed the appropriate numbers into a tiny pad.

Finally, she stepped back. 'OK, I've stored the radio code in this.' She looked at him. 'Shall we use it now?'

Jack shook his head. 'Too risky. We'll come back tonight. Let's go.'

Back upstairs, they hurried through the bookshop and out on to the street.

Hector, Slink and Wren were waiting for them.

'What happened?' Slink said as they walked away.

Jack explained.

'Are we going to break in?' Hector said.

Jack nodded. 'Of course.' His mind raced.

'How exactly are we going to do that?' Slink said.

They turned down an alleyway between two buildings and stopped.

Jack gritted his teeth with determination. 'We have to go back when it's dark.' He looked at Charlie. 'We need supplies. By the time you get to the bunker, I should have a plan.' At least he hoped so.

'I'll be as quick as I can.' Charlie pulled her bandana and hood up, and ran down the alleyway.

When she was gone, Jack turned to Slink. 'Go into the shop and keep an eye out.'

'OK.'

'Let us know if you see anyone suspicious.'

Slink nodded, handed Jack the silver briefcase, winked at Hector, then hurried away.

Jack set the case down by the wall and paced back and forth, thinking. After a minute, he pressed a finger to his ear. 'Obi, can you show me the cameras around the bookshop?'

There was a clicking sound as Obi worked a trackerball. 'Transferring the images to you now.'

Jack pulled his phone from his pocket and looked at the display. It showed four different CCTV camera views from around the area.

Jack squinted. 'Image three,' he said. 'The camera view from behind the bookshop. Is that on a motor-ised mount? Can you tilt the view up?'

'No,' Obi said. 'Look at camera two.'

Jack enlarged the image. It was from a camera further down the road. 'Right. Got it.'

The image panned and tilted until the bookshop came into view again.

'Keep going,' Jack said. 'Show me the roof.'

Obi tilted the view up and stopped. 'That's as far as it goes.'

'That's enough. Can you zoom in?'

Obi did and Jack looked at the chimneys on the roofs either side of the bookshop.

So far, so good.

Jack paced, his mind ablaze.

'What are you thinking?' Hector said. 'Can I help?'

Jack stopped pacing and closed his eyes. He remembered the moment when he and Charlie had first walked into the bookshop.

In his mind's eye he could see every detail – how many steps it took to reach the stairs leading to the basement, the colour of the carpet, the bookshelves, the main gallery at the back of the shop.

There had been a heat sensor above the stained-glass window in the end wall, and an old alarm on the wall in the main shop.

Then Jack remembered the frosted-glass skylights. They were old-fashioned, not double-glazed, and they sat in wooden frames, coated with decades of paint.

There were no catches, no way to open the skylights, but that didn't matter. The fact that there was no way to open them from the inside was a bonus. It meant no alarms to trigger there. They just needed to take care of the heat sensor.

Jack opened his eyes and smiled to himself.

He looked at the time on his phone. They had one hour until the shop closed. Charlie needed to get back here quickly. The sooner they got in and out, the better. Jack typed a message to her, listing everything he needed Charlie to bring back from the bunker.

When he was finished, Jack looked at Wren. 'Do you feel like doing a recon mission?'

She smiled.

• • •

When Charlie came back to the alleyway, she was out of breath and it was twenty minutes past the bookshop's closing time. Slink had already returned and reported that he saw nothing out of the ordinary.

'Come on.' Jack picked up the briefcase, and he, Charlie, Slink and Hector jogged from the alleyway and down the road.

Outside the bookshop, Jack peered through the gaps in the steel shutters. The interior of the shop was dark. Good, the employees had gone home for the night.

He glanced at the shutter over the door. His first thought had been right – it would draw too much attention to try to cut through it. And the alarm would sound before they could deactivate it.

Wren hurried over to them. Her mission had been to check out the rear of the bookshop. She quickly explained that the back door was protected by an isolated CCTV camera.

That meant there was no quick way through there either. So, Jack's original plan was the only chance they had.

Charlie gave a bag to Slink. 'The supplies Jack said you'll need.'

Slink nodded and slipped it over his shoulders.

Jack looked at Charlie, Wren and Hector. 'You three wait here,' he said. 'Keep a lookout.'

'I want to come with you,' Hector said, stepping forward.

'No,' Jack said in a firm tone. 'We'll let you in once we get inside.' He handed Charlie the briefcase and hurried around the corner with Slink.

At the back of the building next door to the bookshop, Jack stood guard while Slink scaled the fence and climbed up using a drainpipe. When he reached the top, he motioned for Jack.

Jack hesitated. He hated heights and climbing, but it needed them both on the roof. For a second, he considered swapping places with Charlie, but he wanted her to keep an eye on Hector.

Jack took a deep breath, used some chalk to dry his hands, then hauled himself over the fence, grabbed the drainpipe and started to climb.

By the time he got to the top, Jack's legs and arms felt like they were on fire. He was breathing heavily and his heart was hammering in his chest.

Slink shook his head. 'You need to go to the gym or something.'

Jack frowned at him, but was too knackered to argue.

Once he'd caught his breath, Jack and Slink scaled the roof of the building, up and over to the bookshop.

They examined the skylight. It was at an angle in the roof and shaped out of eight panes, rising to a peak – four on each side – and the glass was rough and bumpy.

Jack wondered how old it was.

Slink removed a diamond-edged cutter from the bag Charlie had given him, leant over and pressed it to the glass. The diamond tip made a scraping sound and juddered over the surface.

'It's not working,' Slink whispered. 'Glass is too uneven. It won't cut properly.'

Jack scanned the other panes of glass in the skylight. The one in the upper right-hand corner was smooth – a modern replacement. The only problem was Slink would have to climb over the others to get to it.

Jack explained this to him in hurried whispers.

Slink shrugged. 'Guess there's only one way to find out if the glass can hold my weight.'

Jack grimaced at the thought. One false move and Slink would fall into the building. A sliced and diced twelve-year-old would not be a nice thing to have to clean up. Or explain.

Before Jack could stop him, however, Slink lay flat against the lower panels and, with his legs and arms out wide to spread his weight, he slowly, carefully shimmied up the glass.

He was almost at the top pane when there was a *splintering* sound.

Slink froze.

The pane of glass under him fractured into stars and lightning-shaped cracks.

Slink looked at Jack, his eyes wide.

CHAPTER NINE

FOR A LONG MINUTE, NEITHER JACK NOR SLINK moved.

'Ideas?' Slink whispered.

Jack shook his head.

'Great.' Slink composed himself, then edged sideways. The glass cracked again, but he managed to slide his weight off that pane and on to another one.

Jack let out a breath.

Slink continued to move his body up the glass, a millimetre at a time, until finally he reached the top. He pulled the diamond cutter from his pocket and scratched around the outer frame.

'This one seems to be working,' he whispered.

Thank God for that.

Slink used a suction cup, gave the glass a sharp tap and the pane popped out. He carefully lifted it to one side and set it down.

Next, Slink pulled a coil of rope from the back-pack, tied one end through his harness and threw the other to Jack.

Jack hurried over to the chimneys on the other roof, tied the rope around one of them and tugged. He swore.

Slink whispered, 'What's wrong?'

Jack pointed at the chimney. From the camera view Obi had shown him, it had looked strong enough to hold their weight, but several bricks moved when Jack yanked the rope.

He glanced around.

This was not how the mission was supposed to go, but how could he have known there wouldn't be any anchor points up here?

That left only one alternative.

With reluctance, Jack tied the rope around his own waist and braced his feet against the bottom frame of the skylight.

He peered up. The rope would have to slide over the skylight's frame. Was it strong enough to hold Slink's weight?

If the wood was rotten . . .

Slink looked at him. 'Are you sure about this?'

Jack nodded. 'There's a heat sensor just at the corner of the skylight, above the stained-glass window. Use a dark pad.'

Slink hesitated a moment, taking a few deep breaths, then pulled out a telescopic rod with a black piece of tape on the end. He was going to use this to block the sensor's view. 'Right,' he said. 'I'm ready.' And he dropped through the skylight.

Pain instantly tore through Jack's arms and across his back muscles. He fought the urge to cry out. At any moment he expected to hear a popping sound as his shoulders dislocated.

With a supreme effort of willpower, Jack cocked his head to one side and spoke through gritted teeth into the headset, 'Slink?'

'Blocking the heat sensor . . . OK, done. Continuing down.'

Jack squeezed his eyes closed as the pain got worse. 'You nearly there?'

Please let him be nearly there.

'A metre to go.'

Jack shifted his weight.

The pressure suddenly eased.

'I'm down.'

Jack opened his eyes and let out a huge breath.

He lifted each leg until the burning stiffness abated, then circled his arms and shrugged his shoulders up and down.

Finally recovered, Jack untied the rope from his waist. 'Keep an eye out for other sensors. There's an alarm in the main shop. Cut the power to that, then go and open the front door.'

Jack scrambled across the rooftop, slid down the drainpipe and clambered over the fence. By the time he made it to the front of the bookshop, Slink had already deactivated the alarm, picked the lock and was now sliding the shutter up.

He waved Charlie, Wren and Hector through.

'Obi?' Jack whispered into his microphone. 'Is Outlaw World ready?'

'Yes, and the secure phone line.'

'Good. Keep an eye out.'

'Always do.'

Jack glanced up and down the street, then he stepped inside and switched on his torch.

They moved to the back of the darkened book-shop and stood at the top of the stairs. 'The remote,' Jack whispered to Charlie.

She handed him the briefcase and pulled the key fob from her pocket.

'Wait here,' Jack said to Hector, Slink and Wren.

'No way.' Slink headed down the stairs. 'I want to see this hidden Nexus place. It must be amazing.'

'Me too.' Wren hurried after him.

Hector shoved past Jack and followed them down.

Jack looked at Charlie and grumbled as they headed into the basement.

At the back wall, Jack scanned the shelves for any signs of cameras. Spotting none, he nodded at Charlie. 'Do it.'

Charlie pressed the button on the key fob and the whole block of shelves moved out half a metre, then slid aside.

Beyond was a metal door.

Charlie shone her torch on the lock. 'I've got this.' She pulled out a set of picks and got to work.

Suddenly, there was a click.

Charlie straightened up, turned the handle and pulled.

'*No*.' Hector grabbed her arm. 'Look.' He pointed through crack in the door. 'There's an alarm.'

Charlie frowned and shone her torch at it. 'He's right. I haven't seen one of these before.'

'It looks like a new Galloway Alarm.' Hector pointed. 'See that? A feather trigger with a secondary trembler.' He glanced at her. 'Open the door more than a few centimetres and it'll set off the alarm.'

'Any ideas how to get past it?'

'Yes.'

Charlie handed him her torch and stepped back. 'Go for it.'

Jack ground his teeth. 'Don't mess it up.'

'I won't.' Hector turned to Charlie. 'Have you got a long, flatheaded screwdriver?'

Charlie pulled a wallet from her bag and unzipped it. Inside was a range of different screwdrivers.

Before she had a chance, Hector reached over and slid one from its slot. 'I'll also need something sticky.'

'Tape?'

Hector glanced at the door, pulled a stick of chewing gum from his pocket, removed the paper and popped the gum into his mouth.

As he chewed, Hector quickly folded the wrapper into the shape of an elephant and handed it to Wren.

Her eyebrows lifted. 'Thanks. That's cool.'

Hector looked at the others. 'I need a five-pence piece.'

Slink tossed him a coin.

Hector pulled a piece of the gum from his mouth and poked the screwdriver into it.

'Hey,' Charlie whispered, 'that's expensive.'

'I'll clean it after.' Hector fixed the five-pence coin to the chewing gum and turned back to the door.

'What are you doing with that?' Wren said.

Hector glanced at her. 'Stand behind me and I'll show you.'

They watched as Hector carefully slid the screwdriver up and into the gap. The trembler switch moved and Hector froze. When it had stopped vibrating, he continued to push the screwdriver upward. Then, with infinite care, he wedged the five pence behind the two contacts, holding them apart.

Hector reached up and pulled the door open.

'Impressive,' Charlie said.

Hector wiped the screwdriver on his trouser leg and handed it back to her. 'Thanks.'

Slink and Wren gave Jack a look as if to say, *See? Hector's cool* and *clever.*

Jack let out an annoyed breath and shone his torch into the darkened space beyond.

'What the –' Slink whispered. He glanced at Jack. 'That's it?'

The room was empty apart from a chair and table

against the end wall and a high-backed chair in the centre.

Jack found a light switch and flicked it on. A solitary bare bulb hung from the ceiling, glowing a dim yellow.

'Stay here,' he whispered to Slink and Wren.

They both nodded and kept their eyes on the basement stairs.

Jack, Charlie and Hector slipped into the room.

On the wall by the door was a small screen. It showed a view of the other side of the shelves from a hidden camera Jack hadn't seen.

He wondered if there were any other cameras in the building and whether this one was recording, but he doubted it – the image was probably just to show the coast was clear on the other side for when people wanted to leave the room.

He turned around and walked slowly to the chair.

'I was expecting more,' Charlie said.

'Me too.' But it made sense – there wasn't a need for anything else. Jack set down the silver briefcase, opened it and motioned for her.

Charlie walked over and lifted out the glasses. She connected all the wires to the metal box. It seemed to be an input unit that took the signals from the gloves, processed them, then sent them to the Nexus.

Charlie connected an extra cable from the metal box to her phone.

'What's that for?' Hector said.

'We're creating a secure link to one of the bunker's computers,' Charlie said.

'I hope you know what you're doing.'

'Of course we do,' Jack said. 'We're not stupid enough to let the virus escape.' He took the gloves out of the briefcase, pulled them on carefully, then jumped into the chair, while Charlie finished connecting everything.

'Hold up a minute,' Hector said. 'Why do *you* get to go on this?'

'You're only here because I've allowed it,' Jack said, trying to control his temper. 'Count yourself lucky that –'

'Boys,' Charlie hissed. 'Not now.'

'Tell you what then, Hector.' Jack pulled a coin from his pocket. 'Heads I go first, tails, you do. That sound fair?'

Hector shrugged.

Jack threw the coin up, caught it on the back of his hand and showed it to Charlie.

'Heads,' she said.

Hector huffed. 'What a surprise.'

Jack lowered the video glasses over his eyes and a ball of light instantly appeared in front of him. He stared at it, mesmerised.

The ball grew brighter and larger, until it enveloped him in a multicoloured wash of light.

Forms and shapes solidified.

Jack couldn't help but gasp.

'What is it?' Charlie said. 'What do you see?'

'A city.'

Jack was standing on a wide road between shining skyscrapers that stretched to a vibrant blue sky.

He instinctively rotated his hand and pinched his fingers together. The image zoomed in on the individual stones in the road. 'It looks so real.' The hairs on his arms stood on end. 'The resolution is amazing.'

The only thing that gave away that the world wasn't real was that the light seemed slightly artificial, as though everything had a fine aura around it. Also, there was no sound, no wind, no birds, nothing.

'This place is unbelievable.' Jack shook himself. 'Obi?'

'Yeah?'

'Are you seeing this?'

'I can only get a bird's-eye view of the area around you. Can't zoom in or anything. Hold on.' Obi clicked and typed. 'I'm patching the images to your phone, Charlie.'

'Yeah, got it,' she said.

Jack said, 'Obi, is there anyone else here?'

'Not that I can tell.'

'It's hard to see on this small screen,' Charlie said. 'But the place looks empty. No movement.'

'Can you spot anything that might be the virus?'

'No.'

'Obi, they'll have tried to hide it somewhere, so I want you to look for any anomaly that might show us where it is.'

'OK.'

Jack looked up the road, moved his right hand and glided along it, turning his head left and right. There was no reflection of him in the mirrored glass of the buildings and he supposed that was because he didn't have an avatar. Did the people who used this place choose their own? If so, how did they get them?

Moving, however, was second nature to Jack – as if he was born to be part of this world.

A few blocks down, Jack turned a corner and the street opened into a huge open square surrounded by trees.

In the middle was a funfair.

There was a big wheel, a roller coaster and a pirate ship swinging on a great arm. All of them were painted in bright, garish colours – a stark contrast to the modern, clean city around it.

'What's that for?' Charlie said.

'I don't know.' Jack glanced around. It was still eerily quiet. 'Maybe it's part of some kind of anti-terrorist training.'

'It's weird,' Obi said. 'Wait, Jack, there's something in front of you. Inside the funfair.'

Jack looked at the entrance. There was a big banner strung across it that read, *Captain Rat's Wonderland*.

'What do you see?' he said.

'Something shimmering.'

'The virus?'

'I'm not sure.'

Jack took a deep breath and moved towards the entrance.

After a few seconds, he stopped dead in his tracks.

There was a clown with a white face and bright

red hair, standing with his hand raised, as if waving to invisible children.

Jack shuddered, stepped cautiously around him and headed into the funfair.

He followed a brick path that wound its way through the rides – there was a waltzer, bumper cars, shooting galleries and a whole host of other amusements, all of them unmanned and quiet.

Jack kept walking until, in the middle of the funfair, he came across a merry-go-round. 'Obi?'

'The shimmering is right in front of you.'

Jack squinted. 'I can't see anything.' He circled the merry-go-round, looking for any sign of movement.

Something sparkled. Jack stopped and edged closer. One of the horse's ears was made of gold and it glinted in the artificial light.

Jack reached out to touch it and hesitated.

'Wait,' Obi said. 'Do that again.'

Jack stretched out his hand and held it there.

'I can see something change when you do that,' Obi said. 'The top of the merry-go-round shimmers faster.'

Jack stared at the horse's ear as the gold glinted.

He glanced left and right, then touched it.

His fingers vibrated and he quickly pulled his hand back.

'What happened?' Charlie said.

'It's OK.' Jack shook his fingers. 'The gloves have tactile feedback motors in them.'

The merry-go-round started to rotate.

'What's going on?' Obi said.

'I don't know,' Jack said, edging back.

The merry-go-round spun faster and faster, until the horses became a continuous blur of colour.

Jack braced himself, ready to turn and run, but he couldn't take his eyes off it.

The merry-go-round suddenly exploded in a rainbow shower of dust and, where it had once stood, was now a stone archway.

Jack glanced around. The rest of the funfair hadn't changed.

He turned back.

On the other side of the archway was a gravel driveway that led to a timber-framed Tudor house, with white plaster and thick black beams. The upper floor overhung the lower by half a metre or so.

'What's there?' Charlie said.

'A house.'

It was strange – the stone archway stood alone in the centre of the funfair, but through the door, he could see a whole other world.

'Jack,' Obi said. 'We can't see what you're seeing. It just looks black inside.'

'It's some kind of portal,' Jack said. 'Must lead to a hidden part of the Nexus.'

'This place is crazy,' Charlie said.

Jack looked at the front door of the house. 'I'm going for it.' He took a deep breath, stepped through the archway and paused for a couple of seconds. Nothing happened.

'Obi?'

'I can't see where you've gone.'

'Neither can we,' Charlie said.

Jack stepped back. 'See me now?'

'Yes.'

Jack moved through the archway again.

'You've gone again,' Obi said. 'We can't help you. If you stay on that side, you'll be on your own.'

'Understood.' Jack looked left and right. He could see fields and trees in the distance and he relayed this information to the others, narrating as he went. 'The house is just on its own.'

'What are you going to do?' Charlie said.

'I'm going on.' Jack walked toward the house and when he reached the front door, it swung inward.

'What's happening?' Charlie said. 'What do you see?'

'Nothing.' Jack shook off the feeling of foreboding and stepped inside.

Beyond was a narrow hallway with stairs and a wooden floor. Several oil paintings hung on the walls – they were all portraits, but Jack didn't recognise any of the people in them.

He looked around. There was a door to his left and one on the right. He had no idea which way to go, so he moved to the door on the left and, like the front door, it opened automatically. 'It's a dining room.'

'Why's there a dining room?' Hector said. 'What's the point of that?'

It was a low-ceilinged room with a table and six chairs in the centre. The table was laid with silver plates and cutlery.

Jack turned around, walked across the hallway and went through the other door.

Beyond was a cozy sitting room. Two chairs sat facing a fireplace. Flames flickered in the hearth and, for the first time, Jack heard a sound – the crackle of burning wood.

'There's nothing here either.' He was about to turn away when something shimmered in the corner of his eye. Jack spun back. Now he looked, he could see the fire was changing colour, pulsating, almost dancing.

Jack took a step towards it and continued to stare at the fire as small lightning bolts rippled over its surface.

He crouched in front of it. Letters, numbers and symbols danced with the flames. 'I think I've found the virus,' he said. 'Obi, open the door to Outlaw World.'

Outlaw World was their own virtual environment. Jack and Obi had designed it to test missions, but they'd never got around to using it. Outlaw World was nothing more than a blank space. That didn't matter though – they just needed an empty world to put the virus in. A way to contain it. Then, once it was inside, Obi would shut Outlaw World down before the virus could cause any damage to their computers.

'I've made the door,' Obi said. 'Connected the Nexus and Outlaw World together, but I can't get it close to you.'

'Where is it?' Jack said.

203

'Near where you first appeared – in the middle of the road. Something's stopping me moving the door any closer.'

Jack leant in to the virus. 'I can see the code,' he breathed. The programming language looked like Python mixed with Ruby, but it was different some-how, as though it had evolved into something more advanced.

'Jack?'

He watched as a blue streak of numbers and let-ters zigzagged over the surface of the virus.

'*Jack*,' Charlie shouted.

He almost leapt out of the chair. 'What?'

'Find a way to get the virus out of there. Take it to the door.'

Jack broke his gaze and looked left and right, examining the room closely. 'I can't see a way.'

'Let me try,' Hector said.

'No.' Jack reached out and the virus vibrated under his touch. He then cupped his hands around it and backed up. The virus came with him. 'I can carry it.' Jack turned to the door, walked into the hallway and back outside.

He glided down the path, holding the pulsating virus out in front of him.

Jack hesitated when he reached the archway. He could see the funfair on the other side, but would the Nexus allow him to take the virus through there?

Only one way to find out.

Jack tensed and stepped over the threshold.

The virus came with him.

He smiled. 'I'm on my way.'

'We see you again,' Obi said.

Jack walked back through the funfair and as he passed under the main entrance and out on to the street, he said, 'Obi, is the door still there?'

'Yes. We have a secure link to Outlaw World.'

Jack continued down the road and turned the corner.

Ahead, he could see a large green door – his target.

'Jack,' Charlie cried. 'Look out.'

Something shot past Jack's line of sight, almost knocking the virus from his hands.

He looked back to see the clown, its face twisted into rage, swinging its arms in an attempt to grab the virus.

Jack turned and pushed forward as hard as he could.

'Hurry,' Obi said.

Ahead, the green door opened in anticipation. On the other side was a black and white checkerboard – Outlaw World.

Suddenly, the clown lashed out and knocked the virus from Jack's hands. He went to pick it up again, but the clown beat him to it and backed towards the funfair, holding the virus close to its chest.

Jack made to follow, but the clown's face turned as red as its hair and an alarm blasted his eardrums.

'I've lost the connection,' Obi said.

Jack looked at the door as it vanished and the world around him faded to black.

He reached up and yanked the goggles from his head. 'They're on to us.' He climbed out of the chair and quickly pulled off the gloves, swearing under his breath.

So close.

'You should have let me do it,' Hector shouted.

Jack wheeled on him. *'Shut up.'*

'What now?' Charlie said.

'I don't know.' Jack looked around the sparse room. 'Let me think.'

'We don't have time for that.' Hector marched

behind the chair and grabbed Charlie's phone. It was still connected to the Nexus, and he quickly typed.

'What do you think you're doing?' Jack said, trying to snatch it from him.

'Correcting your mistake.' Hector pressed the Send button.

Slink stuck his head around the door. 'Are we getting out of here or what?'

'Just a few more seconds,' Hector said, his eyes glued to the display on Charlie's phone.

'We don't have a few seconds.' Jack yanked the cable out. 'Go. *Now.*'

'You idiot,' Hector shouted. 'I almost had that.'

'You had nothing,' Jack said. 'Get. Out.'

Hector looked as though he wanted to punch Jack square in the face, but instead he turned and ran from the room.

Charlie shoved the glasses, gloves and metal box into the briefcase and scooped it up in her arms. 'No way I'm leaving this here.'

The others followed Hector up the stairs and through the shop.

Back outside, they heard the distant sound of police sirens.

Slink pulled the shutters into place and they jogged down the road.

A car screeched to a halt behind them.

Jack glanced over his shoulder to see a man in a dark suit leap out and sprint to the front of the shop. He fumbled with a set of keys in his hand.

Jack and the others turned into the alley.

When they were a safe distance away, Charlie said, 'Is that it then? It's over?'

'We triggered the alarm,' Jack said. 'They know someone was trying to hack into the Nexus. They'll shut down all the access points.'

'There has to be another way,' Slink said.

Jack didn't answer. The truth was, there wasn't another way. Well, not one he could think of.

'It's your fault,' Hector said, turning on him. 'If you'd let me go into the Nexus, we'd have the virus by now.'

'It's your fault it leaked back to the internet,' Jack said. 'If it wasn't for you, we wouldn't even be here.'

Charlie scowled at Jack and rested a hand on Hector's shoulder. 'We don't blame you. You weren't to know.'

'It was nice meeting you.' Hector shook every-one's hands apart from Jack's. 'If you're ever around my neighbourhood . . .' He glanced at Jack one more time, then walked away.

Jack let him go – there was no reason to keep Hector close any more. Who cared if he told someone about the Nexus? It didn't matter now.

Charlie said to Jack, 'Are you sure there's no other way to get the virus?'

'No. As soon as they realise what's happened, they'll shut down all the Nexus's access points and double the security.' Jack pulled his hood up and bowed his head.

It was over.

CHAPTER TEN

JACK, CHARLIE, SLINK AND WREN FOLLOWED THE old stone tunnel that led to the bunker.

Wren hurried alongside Jack. 'I like him,' she said.

Jack glanced at her. 'Who?'

'Hector.'

'Oh.' Jack kept his pace up.

'Hey,' Slink said. 'Why don't we show him the bunker?'

Jack reached the outer airlock door and turned back to stare at him. 'Are you crazy? We can't trust him.' He grabbed the handle and swung the door open.

'Why not?' Wren said as she, Slink and Charlie stepped into the airlock corridor.

'Because,' Jack said, joining them, 'we've known Hector less than a day.'

'He saved Slink's life,' Wren said. 'Anyway, Charlie brought me here when she first met me. Right, Charlie?'

Charlie nodded.

'Yeah, well, that's different,' Jack said. 'You're just a –'

Wren scowled. 'Just a what?'

Jack hesitated, glanced at Charlie and sighed. 'We can't trust him, all right?'

Slink waved at the camera and typed the code into the keypad. The door slid open. 'I say we vote on it.'

The others hurried after him.

'Vote? Vote on what exactly?'

'Whether we should let Hector be part of our group or not.'

Jack's eyes widened at that. 'We are *not* making him one of us. No way.' This was getting out of hand – they'd only been discussing whether they should allow Hector to see the bunker. This was ridiculous.

'We could use him,' Wren said. 'He's got all sorts of skills.'

Slink strode over to Obi. 'What do you think? Should we let Hector join the Urban Outlaws?'

Obi's eyes wandered to the ceiling as he

considered this. Finally, he looked at Jack. 'I'm not sure.'

'Thank you,' Jack said. 'At least someone sees sense.'

'*Obi*,' Wren moaned.

'What? He's a stranger.'

'No he's not,' Wren said. 'A stranger is someone you've never met. We've already met Hector, haven't we?'

Slink grinned. 'Can't argue with that.'

Obi pointed at the screens. 'I can watch him for a while, if you like? See what he gets up to. And . . .' He clicked the trackerball and brought up a window. 'I've done that digging you asked me to do.'

Wren put her hands on her hips and looked at Jack. 'You've been spying on Hector?'

'Background check,' Jack said.

'Hector's been going to Granger High for the past few years.' Obi clicked and another window popped up. 'See? His dad is a salesman and his mum died a few years ago.'

'So, what else did you find out?' Slink said. 'Is Hector an axe murderer or something?'

'No. He's just a normal kid.'

'He's not normal,' Wren said. 'He's really clever.'

Charlie looked at Jack. 'That fits in with what he told us.'

'Not you too,' Jack said.

Charlie held her hands up. 'Just saying.'

• • •

The next morning, Jack sat on one of the sofas in the lounge area of the bunker and thought about everything that had happened so far.

The government would now be in the process of dissecting the virus to see how it worked, and once they'd figured it out, they'd have the world's best hacking tool at their disposal.

How long would it be before they worked out how to copy the virus? How long before they started stealing secrets and controlling the internet? No hacker would be safe, and neither would the Urban Outlaws. One false move and the government would track down the bunker.

Jack buried his head in his hands and his thoughts turned to Hector.

Was the reason that Jack was so wary of him because he was jealous of Hector? Did Jack see him as a threat? He had to admit it was impressive the way Hector had beaten them to the virus at the power station. The way he slipped past them all. And they could use someone with his skills on their team. A good all-rounder.

But Hector wasn't *that* clever, Jack reminded himself. He did let the virus slip through his firewalls.

There was a screeching sound and Wren shot from the corridor, across the bunker, hit the sofa opposite Jack and went flying over the top of it.

Charlie ran into the room and glanced around. 'Wren?'

A hand rose into the air.

Charlie hurried behind the sofa. 'Are you OK?' she said, helping Wren to her feet.

Wren wobbled and grabbed the back of the sofa for support.

'What are you two doing?' Jack said.

Wren edged her way around the sofa and pointed at her feet. She was wearing a pair of Rollerblades.

Slink sat at the dining table. He held up a piece of paper with a large number seven on it. 'I would've given you eight out of ten,' he said, 'but I knocked off a point for the landing.'

'Why are you showing her how to skate?' Jack asked Charlie.

'More like, "how to crash",' Obi said.

Slink snorted.

'She's just having a bit of fun after that last mission.' Charlie looked at Jack. 'I wouldn't mind doing something fun myself, come to think of it.'

Jack nodded and stood up. 'You're right. And I have an idea for a mission we can *all* do.' He turned around. 'Obi?'

'Yeah?'

'Charlie says you've got the plans to another one of your old houses. Can we have a look?'

Obi's eyes lit up. 'Are you serious?'

'Yeah, serious.' Jack strode over to Obi's chair.

Slink said to Obi, 'Before we go through this again, are you sure there's another will? Like, *really*, *really* positive?'

'I know there is,' Obi said with complete conviction. He brought up the architectural plans to the house on the main monitor.

Jack stared, stunned by what he was looking at. The house was actually a mansion with nine bedrooms, seven bathrooms, five reception rooms and two separate offices, all spread over three floors, including a basement. The house even had its own lift.

Jack glanced at the others – they had the same look of astonishment on their faces.

'Hey, Obi,' Slink said, his mouth still hanging open. 'You actually lived there?' He glanced around the bunker. 'It makes this place look like a sh–'

'*Shack*,' Charlie interrupted.

'Yeah,' Slink said. 'Exactly what I was going to say. "Shack." Makes this place look like a shack.' He winked at Wren and she grinned.

'Wait a minute,' Jack said, leaning into the screen and squinting at the bottom-right corner where the architect had written the name of the house. Jack stood straight and looked at Obi. 'Where exactly is this?'

Obi glanced away and fiddled with his fingers.

'Obi,' Jack said. 'Where is this house?'

Obi let out a breath. 'France.'

'Ha,' Slink said, throwing his hands in the air. 'That's really brilliant. How are we supposed to get to France?'

Jack frowned at the plans. The mansion was called Chateau Gailan. 'Whereabouts in France is it?' he asked.

'Around sixty kilometres from Calais.'

'Oh, that's all right then,' Slink said. 'I'll just go

get my passport.' He walked away and stopped. 'Wait a tick.' He turned back. 'I just remembered, I don't actually *have* a passport.'

Jack started to pace back and forth, his mind searching for answers.

'I don't have a passport either,' Wren said.

'None of us do,' Charlie said.

'I have,' Jack said.

Charlie frowned at him. 'How come?'

'You remember. A few years ago my class went on a school trip to Belgium.'

'Well,' Slink said, leaning against a pillar, 'send us a postcard.'

'I thought you were British,' Wren said to Obi, looking confused.

'It was my mum and dad's summer house,' Obi said.

'Wow,' Wren said. 'That's just the summer house?'

'We lived in Windsor most of the time,' Obi said. 'Mum and Dad used the apartment in London for when they had to stay over for business meetings.'

'Three houses?' Wren muttered. 'Who needs three houses?'

Obi shrugged and looked a little embarrassed. 'I

know there's a good chance my dad would've had a copy of the will in France.'

Charlie looked at Jack. 'Is there a way for us all to do this?'

A wry smile spread across his face. 'There is one way.'

Slink groaned as he caught on to what Jack was planning. 'I've got a feeling this is going to be a pain. Literally.'

Wren's eyes lit up. 'Are we really going to France? Really? I've never been to another country.'

Jack looked at Obi. 'We're *all* going.' Next, he looked at Charlie. 'Including Robbie.'

• • •

Four hours later, Jack was sitting in the passenger seat of a white and pink ice-cream van, watching the border security on the Calais side of the Channel go by.

No one stopped them or searched the van.

When they were a mile or so away from Chateau Gailan, Noble glanced in the rear-view mirror. 'OK,' he said. 'I think it's time to check on our passengers.

Jack climbed out of his seat, walked to the back

of the van and pulled a blind down, blocking the view of the people in the car behind.

He turned around. 'It's safe.'

The handle on the ice-cream machine clicked and the whole front of it swung open.

Slink stepped out and cricked his neck. 'Are we in France yet?'

'Yes.'

Slink breathed out a sigh of relief.

Next to the ice-cream machine, a tall cupboard door opened and Charlie climbed out. 'That was fun . . . *Not*.' She frowned. 'Where's Wren?'

Jack knelt down and slid open a door to the cupboard under the sink.

Wren was curled up inside, fast asleep.

Jack shook her and she stirred.

Finally, Wren clambered out to join the others.

Slink looked around. 'I feel like we're forgetting something.' There was a muffled cry from the chest freezer. Slink sat on the lid. 'Nah, maybe not. So, have we got anything to drink?'

Jack shoved Slink off the freezer and opened it.

A round face and two large eyes blinked up at him.

'Get. Me. Out.'

'Hey,' Slink said. 'It could've been worse – at least it wasn't switched on.'

'Not funny.'

With a lot of effort, Jack and Slink helped pull Obi out of the freezer.

He staggered and steadied himself. 'I'm never getting back in there again.'

'I hate to break it to you, mate,' Jack said, 'but we'll have to do the same thing going home.'

Obi groaned.

• • •

It was getting dark by the time they finally found Chateau Gailan. It sat on a hill, surrounded by a high brick wall topped with metal spikes.

Noble pulled the ice-cream van off the main road and parked next to a small wooded area.

'Right,' Slink said to Jack. 'Now what?'

Jack looked at Obi. 'Where do you think the will is?'

'In a safe, in my dad's office.'

Charlie rolled her eyes. 'Another safe?'

'It's OK,' Obi said. 'This one is old. It has one of those dials on it.'

'Can you crack it?' Jack asked Charlie.

'Yeah, no problem.'

Jack turned back to Obi. 'Tell us about the security.'

Obi peered out of the window at the mansion, as though he were recalling something deep in his past. After a minute, he turned back. 'My dad's office was at the back, far-right corner.'

Jack nodded, remembering the plans that he'd now committed to memory. 'Are you sure your uncle won't be here?'

'Yes,' Obi said. 'I checked before we left the bunker – he was at the apartment in Hyde Park.'

'OK,' Jack said, looking out the window at the mansion. 'Will there be anyone else around?'

Obi shook his head. 'Don't think so.'

'We should scope the place out to be sure.' Jack gestured to Obi and Charlie. 'Time for Robbie.'

'Ah, Robbie,' Noble said with obvious fondness. 'He has proven his worth so many times.'

Wren frowned at him. 'Who?'

Obi slid a netbook from his bag. It had two joysticks and an antenna on the back. It was the same one Jack had used to control Shadow Bee – the remote-controlled stealth helicopter – on a previous mission.

Obi made sure the netbook was up and running, then looked at Charlie. 'All set.'

Charlie reached into her bag. 'Wren, meet Robbie.' She pulled out a radio-controlled vehicle, eight centimetres high, twelve wide and twenty long. It had tank tracks either side and two tiny cameras mounted on the front that made it look as if it had a face.

Wren stared. She seemed unsure what to make of it. '*This* is Robbie?'

'Yep.' Charlie flicked on a switch and set Robbie down on the floor.

Everyone gathered around Obi.

He typed a few commands. 'Connected.'

An image flickered on the netbook screen. It was Robbie's view of the world – bathed in green nightvision.

Obi touched the mouse pad and pushed his finger forward. Robbie also moved forward. Obi swept his finger left and right. Robbie followed his commands. Obi stopped and looked at Jack. 'All good.'

'OK,' Jack said. 'Let's go have a look.'

Noble opened the passenger door and set Robbie down outside.

Obi pushed his finger forward and Robbie raced through the trees.

Wren gasped. 'He's fast.'

Robbie weaved between the trunks, rolled up a fallen log, jumped into the air and landed on a dirt track.

'Woohoo,' Obi shouted.

'Shhh,' Jack hissed, waving for Noble to shut the door again.

Obi guided Robbie along the outer wall. 'Up here there's another way into the grounds. Ten metres or so. It's the only way through, apart from the main entrance.'

A little while later, Robbie stopped outside a gate in the wall and turned to face it.

'Can you scan that?' Jack said.

Obi tilted the cameras up. There was an old-fashioned lock in the ironwork, but it also had a thick padlock and chain.

'I can get through,' Charlie said. 'But I'll have to use a saw.'

'That's no good,' Jack said. 'Sawing will attract too much attention.'

'Can you tilt the camera up a bit more?' Noble said.

Obi pulled back on one of the joysticks and the camera moved up.

There was no way through.

'I can get over that,' Slink said.

'*You* might be able to,' Jack said, 'but the rest of us can't. How are we going to get in?'

'Hinges,' Charlie said.

They all looked at her.

'Show me the hinges.'

The image turned to the left and moved down the gate.

Charlie pointed. 'That's the weak point. I can break through those silently.' She rifled through her bag and pulled out a thick, flat iron bar. She stood up. 'Give me five minutes.'

'I'll come with you,' Slink said.

They climbed out of the van and disappeared through the trees.

Noble was now sitting in the driver's seat, making sure no one was watching them.

Jack kept his attention on the netbook display and a couple of minutes later Charlie and Slink jogged into view.

Slink leapt up the gate and scaled the wall. He held on to the spikes and peered into the garden. He gave Charlie a thumbs-up and she set to work.

She jammed the iron bar between the hinge and

wall and pulled. After a few seconds, she shook her head and tried again, this time bracing her feet against the brickwork.

She yanked hard and stumbled back.

Robbie shifted position and they could see Charlie had broken the first hinge off.

She knelt down and jammed the bar behind the second hinge. She glanced up at Slink, then heaved. The second hinge came away more easily.

Charlie turned, grinned into the camera and swung the gate open.

Slink jumped down and the two of them stared into the garden.

'It all looks quiet,' Charlie whispered.

Without hesitation, and before the other two got any ideas, Jack asked Obi to guide Robbie through the gate and over the lawn towards the house.

A couple of minutes later, the van door opened and Charlie and Slink climbed back in.

'I thought for a minute that you two were going to look at the house,' Jack said.

'We did consider it,' Charlie said. 'It seems deserted.'

Jack glanced at the display – sure enough, there

were no lights on. The house was completely dark. Chateau Gailan was indeed empty.

But they couldn't be too careful. Besides, just because no one was home, didn't mean there wasn't any other security, like cameras, watching them.

Obi guided Robbie along a gravel path and around to the rear of the mansion.

A manicured lawn stretched into the distance, flanked by sculpted hedgerows. In the centre was a large circular fountain.

Obi stopped Robbie and hesitated.

'What's wrong?' Jack said.

'I'm not sure of the best way to go.' He swung the camera to the back door. 'Either through the pantry, down the hallway, then to Dad's old office or . . .' He pointed the camera to the right side of the building and aimed it at a tall window, 'we just go straight through that way.'

Jack looked at Charlie. 'Ideas?'

She leant over Obi's shoulder and peered at the image. 'Is there a burglar alarm?'

'I think so.'

'Where is it?'

'The keypad is by the front door.'

Charlie sat back. 'Can I see the office window?'

Obi guided Robbie to the window and panned the camera up and down. From their viewpoint, they couldn't see any other signs of security.

No wires.

No sensors.

Nothing.

Charlie frowned. 'OK, go to the front of the house.'

Obi steered Robbie down the side of the building and round to the front. It had a large impressive oak door with a brass knocker and handle.

There was still no sign of security and Robbie was too low to the ground to get a good look through the windows.

Jack glanced at Charlie. 'Well?'

She shrugged. 'I don't know, Jack. We could just go for it.'

Jack cocked an eyebrow at her. 'OK, which way then? Office window or front door?'

'Both.' Noble turned in his seat to look at them. 'Go both ways.'

'He's right,' Jack said. 'Charlie has the best chance at deactivating the alarm control panel. I'll go with her through the front door. Meantime, Slink and Wren can get into the office through the window at the back and see if the safe is in there. That way, if Charlie has any problems with the alarm, we'll still have got a good look at the place.' He turned to Obi. 'Use Robbie to patrol the grounds. Any movement, let us know.'

Charlie handed them all headsets.

'I'll stay and keep an eye out here,' Noble said. 'Make sure we don't get any unwanted visitors.'

'Me too,' Obi said. 'I'll use Robbie to patrol the grounds.'

Jack, Charlie, Slink and Wren climbed out of the ice-cream van and hurried through the trees.

They reached the gate and jogged silently across the lawn.

When they got to the house, Jack and Charlie headed to the front door, while Slink and Wren ran round the back.

Once everyone was in position Jack spoke into his headset. 'Slink, can you see any security now you have a better view?'

There was a short pause before Slink said, 'Yeah. There's a sensor on this window.'

Jack looked at Charlie. 'Well?'

Charlie cupped her hands over the glass panel in the front door and peered into the hallway. 'I can see the alarm on the wall.' She swore under her breath.

'What's wrong?' Jack said.

'It's old. Never seen that type before.'

'Old is good though, right?' Jack said. 'Isn't it easier to crack?'

'I'm used to systems that are a little more advanced.' Charlie pulled back, slid a wallet of lock picks from her bag and set to work on the front door.

Jack pressed a finger to his ear. 'Slink?'

'I can get this window open easily. No problems.'

'Wait until we say.' Jack glanced around to make doubly sure there were no cameras.

There was a click as Charlie unlocked the door. She straightened up.

Jack nodded at her. 'Go.'

She opened the door and the beeps from the alarm started. Charlie jogged over to the panel.

'Go, Slink,' Jack said into his microphone, and he hurried in after her.

Charlie was right – the alarm box on the wall had huge grey buttons and looked like an antique typewriter.

The beeps started speeding up.

'So?' Jack said, looking between Charlie and the panel.

Charlie pulled off the cover and peered inside at

the components. She frowned, muttering under her breath as her eyes traced the paths of the wires.

The beeps grew faster.

How much time did they have left? Twenty seconds? Ten?

'Would you like some help?'

Jack leapt back and spun around.

Noble strode over to them. 'Ah, the Go-Secure two-thousand,' he said. 'I remember when these first came out.' He glanced at Charlie. 'May I?'

Charlie stepped aside.

The beeps were so fast now that it would be only a matter of seconds before the alarm went off.

'They don't make them like this any more,' Noble said, peering inside the box.

Jack's stomach knotted.

Noble cleared his throat. 'Now, let's see.' He gripped either side with both hands. The rapid beeps turned into one long tone. With a swift movement, Noble ripped the box off the wall, breaking all the wires and bringing a chunk of plaster with it.

Jack stared in disbelief.

Noble glanced up at the ceiling and listened for a moment. Finally, he said, 'That should do it,' and tossed the alarm box out of the front door and on to the gravel driveway. Noble bowed. 'See you back at the van,' he said and strode from the house.

Jack had to snap himself back to reality. 'Slink?' he whispered into his headset.

'We've found the –' Slink hesitated. 'Erm, safe?'

Jack and Charlie hurried down the corridor and through the last door on the right.

The office was wood-panelled and several oil paintings hung on the walls. A large desk sat next to the window.

Slink had pulled back one of the wood panels from the wall to reveal a metal door, two metres tall, one wide, with a large dial in the centre and a handle.

'That's not a safe,' Charlie said. 'That's a flipping vault.'

There was a scraping sound and Jack wheeled around as Robbie came trundling into the room.

Jack said into his microphone, 'Obi, you're supposed to be patrolling the perimeter.'

'I had to see.'

Robbie's camera tilted up.

Jack walked over to the vault door and stood next to Charlie.

She knelt down and unzipped her bag. She put on a pair of headphones that were attached to a microphone inside a suction cup. She pressed the cup to the vault door and started to rotate the dial slowly.

Charlie closed her eyes as she listened to the mechanism inside.

Jack held his breath.

Charlie stopped and mouthed the number 'nine' to him. She then turned the dial slowly the other way and stopped again.

'Twenty-seven.'

She rotated the dial back in the opposite direction.

'Seventeen.'

There was a click.

She grabbed the handle and unlocked the door.

Charlie put the microphone and headphones back in her bag and stood up.

Jack glanced at the others, then swung the vault door fully open.

It was empty.

Nothing but bare shelves.

Robbie rolled forward and the camera looked from left to right, up and down.

'Well, that's just brilliant.' Slink leant into Robbie's camera, his face a few centimetres away. 'Empty again.'

'We have company,' Noble said in their ears. 'Main driveway.'

Jack spun around. 'Get out of here,' he said to the others and he sprinted from the office and down the hallway.

He reached the front door and peered out in time to see a car coming up the driveway.

CHAPTER ELEVEN

THE CAR FOLLOWED THE CURVE OF THE DRIVEWAY, heading straight towards the house.

Jack pressed a finger to his ear. 'Obi, who's this?'

'My uncle.'

'What? I thought you said he was in London?'

'He was.'

Jack glanced at the burglar alarm box on the ground in front of the steps. There wasn't enough time to grab it and get back inside without being seen.

He slammed the front door shut and ran down the hallway. When he got to the office, he was stunned to see Charlie was still there.

'What are you doing?' he said. 'Get out of here.'

'Wait a minute.' Charlie turned slowly on the spot, her eyes narrowed and scanning the room. 'It has to be here somewhere. I know it.'

'What are you on about? We have to go.'

'No,' Charlie waved a finger at the vault. 'This can't be where he kept a copy of the will.'

'Why not?'

'Because Obi said his dad never trusted his uncle.' Charlie's eyes moved around the room, still searching for something.

'Charlie, we don't have time for this.' Jack grabbed her arm, but she pulled away from him.

She ran to the far side of the room and lifted a painting of an old boat from the wall. She looked behind it, then lowered it back into place and moved to a portrait of a French general.

'Hey, guys?' Obi said through the headset. 'What's going on?'

Jack didn't respond. He was rooted to the spot, watching Charlie.

She ran her fingers around the portrait of the general, muttering to herself.

Jack heard a car door slam.

Charlie cursed and moved to a set of shelves. She lifted a few books and examined them before putting them back.

'*Charlie.*'

She held up a hand. 'Just a few seconds.'

Jack heard the distant sound of someone fumbling with a set of keys. 'We don't have a few seconds.' He hurried over to the office door, closed and locked it, then turned back.

Charlie was now sitting behind the desk. She opened all the drawers on the left, before moving to the right-hand side. She then slid open the top drawer and ran her finger under the edge of the work surface. 'Yes.' There was a small click as she pressed a button. She slid open a hidden compartment. 'Knew it.'

Jack stared, dumbfounded, as she lifted out a stack of papers and envelopes and started rifling through them.

The front door slammed. *'Who's there?'*

'Time's up,' Jack said.

Charlie continued flicking through the papers, scanning the titles.

There was the sound of running footsteps in the hallway.

Finally, Charlie opened a Manila envelope, scanned over the contents and stuffed it all under her jacket. She stood up.

The office door rattled.

'Who's in there? I've called the police.'

They ran to the window and Jack helped Charlie out.

The office door burst open and a tall man stood silhouetted in the light from the hall. He stepped into the room and Jack could see his face clearly now – it was twisted in rage. Jack recognised Obi's uncle. His eyes locked on to Jack's and he lunged forward, hands outstretched.

Jack spun clear and leapt out of the window.

Obi's uncle roared.

Jack and Charlie sprinted down the path, across the lawn and through the side gate. They stayed close to the wall. When they got back to the road, the ice-cream van had gone.

Jack spun on the spot, searching for it. 'Where are they?'

Charlie grabbed his shoulder and pointed. '*There.*'

The ice-cream van came screaming down the road towards them.

Jack stared. 'What is Noble doing?'

Suddenly, the van veered off the road and hit the front gates at an angle, buckling them.

'He's gone crazy,' Charlie said, open-mouthed.

'No,' Jack said. 'Look.' The van backed up. The iron gates to the driveway were bent and misshapen.

'Now there's no way for Obi's uncle to chase us.'

'Don't be so sure,' Charlie said, sprinting towards the van and gesturing over her shoulder.

Jack glanced back.

Obi's uncle was running towards them. 'Get back here,' he shouted.

Jack spun around, ran over to the van and climbed in. 'Hurry.'

Noble slammed the ice-cream van into first gear. 'I thought I was buying us a little time. Seems I was wrong.'

Through the windscreen, Jack could see Obi's uncle still running at them like a T. rex hunting its prey.

'He looks determined,' Slink said.

Jack glanced back at Obi. 'Don't let him see you.'

Obi ducked out of sight.

There was a loud thud and Jack turned back.

Obi's uncle was spread-eagled across the van's bonnet, foaming at the mouth and staring through the windscreen at them like a rabid animal.

Noble wrestled with the ice-cream van's gear stick and reversed back up the road, but Obi's uncle held on.

Charlie leant over and turned on the windscreen

wipers. They swished back and forth, slapping Obi's uncle in the face, but he still clung on. With each pass of the wiper, he looked even more annoyed.

If that was possible.

Noble slammed on the brakes, threw the van into first again and accelerated down the road with Obi's uncle still clinging to the bonnet.

'He doesn't give up, does he?' Charlie said.

'I'll get him off,' Slink said, climbing out of the side window before Jack could stop him.

Jack looked out through the windscreen.

A few seconds later, a foot came down on Obi's uncle's hands.

He roared again, with what Jack assumed to be a mixture of pain and rage.

The foot came down again and Obi's uncle tried to grab it, but he missed. The foot swung in from the left, hitting him in the temple.

Obi's uncle screamed out in pain and his grip slipped.

Noble saw his chance. 'Hold on Slink,' he yelled out of the window, then yanked the steering wheel hard over.

Obi's uncle slipped past the windscreen and vanished.

Jack glanced through the rear window and watched as he rolled down the road.

Obi's uncle then got to his knees and shook a fist at them as they disappeared around the corner.

Wren shouted.

Jack spun around. 'What?'

She pointed.

Slink was hanging upside down outside the open side window.

Jack and Charlie leapt over and grabbed him.

'My trousers are caught on the ice-cream sign,' Slink said. 'Have you got me?'

Jack made sure he had a good grip on Slink's belt. 'I think so.'

Slink shifted his weight and rolled backward.

His foot sprang free and Jack and Charlie pulled him through the window.

They hit the floor, panting.

Slink grinned.

Charlie punched his arm.

• • •

When they were several kilometres from Chateau Gailan, Charlie removed the Manila envelope from under her jacket and handed it to Obi. 'Is this what you wanted?'

Obi's eyes went wide. With shaking fingers, he slid out the sheets of paper and scanned the pages.

Finally, he looked up at the others.

'Well?' Charlie said.

'It's Dad's real will.' Obi's eyes welled up, but he didn't cry. He looked at them all. 'Thanks,' he said, his voice cracking.

• • •

On the journey back through the Channel Tunnel, Obi remained silent. He held the Manila envelope in his hand and stared at it.

'Well, come on then,' Slink said eventually.

Obi looked up. 'What?'

Slink rolled his eyes. 'We travelled all that way. Nearly got caught – several times – and not to mention the fact that I'm going to have stiff muscles for a week. The least you could do is tell us what it says.'

Obi held the envelope out to Charlie.

'You want me to read it?' she said.

He nodded.

Charlie slid the paperwork out and cleared her throat. 'The last will and testament of Mark Brian

242

Harlington. I revoke all previous wills and codicils.'
Charlie glanced up at Obi, then continued to read. 'I
appoint as executor and trustee of my will Antony
James Harlington.' Her eyes skimmed down the
page. 'Your mum and dad also made him your legal
guardian. Wait a minute . . .' She looked up at Obi.
'You were right – they left the business and all assets
to you and your sister.'

'How can that be right?' Slink said. 'He's only a kid.'

Charlie continued to read. 'It says here that Obi's
sister is supposed to run the business until Obi's
eighteen, then they share the responsibility.'

'Read the bit about my uncle,' Obi said in a flat
tone.

Charlie read some more, then looked up. Her
eyes were full of compassion. 'He was left fifty thousand pounds and a Rolls Royce. He was never
supposed to inherit anything else. You and your
sister are the rightful heirs.' She slid the will back
into the envelope and handed it to Obi.

Obi stared down at it.

'I suggest everyone returns to their hiding places,'
Noble said. 'We're nearly back in England.'

• • •

Noble drove off the train, followed the signs and they reached the last checkpoint. The bored man behind the glass glanced over Jack and Noble's passports, then handed them back.

The barrier lifted and Noble went to pull forward but another border official stepped into their path, holding up his hand.

Noble leant out of the side window. 'Is there a problem?'

The man's eyes narrowed as he took in the dents and the scratches on the ice-cream van's bonnet and bumper. With a stern expression, he pointed to the side, where two more men in border agency uniforms were waiting. 'Pull over there please.'

Jack's heart sank.

Noble edged the van forward.

Jack glanced at him. It was clear that Noble was considering making a break for it, but they'd never get away, especially in an ice-cream van.

Noble pulled up as instructed. The two men started walking around the van, checking underneath with mirrors on poles.

'Nobody breathe,' Noble hissed over his shoulder.

The first border official stood in front of the van,

inspecting the dents. He then walked around to Noble's window. 'How did you get those?'

'I came off the road avoiding a collision,' Noble said. 'Hit a tree.'

The man frowned. 'Are you American, sir?'

'Yes.' Noble smiled at him. 'Though I am now also a fully fledged citizen of the United Kingdom.'

The border official looked at the dents again.

Even Jack had to admit it appeared like they'd hit a lot more than just a tree.

The man held out his hand and said, 'Passports, please.'

Noble gestured behind them. 'We just showed them back there.'

The official's eyes narrowed. 'Passports.'

Noble sighed and handed them to him.

The man took a long time checking them over, his face close to each picture page as if trying to detect whether the passports were forgeries or not.

The men with mirrors were now on their second sweep around the van.

Jack's stomach tightened. It was as if they knew Noble and Jack were hiding something.

Jack tried to relax and show no outward sign of his anxiety.

Finally, the border official handed the passports to Noble. 'How long were you in France?'

'Less than a day.'

'What were you doing there?'

'Sightseeing.'

'What sights?'

'We saw a chateau.'

'A chateau? Which one?'

Noble looked puzzled. 'I forget its name.'

The two men stopped and stood by the front of the van.

'Nothing underneath. Do you want us to take a look inside?'

The first border official was looking distractedly into the distance. Jack followed his gaze to the barrier, where a bearded man in a white van was having an animated argument with the officer behind the window.

The border official glanced over at Jack, then into the back of the van, then waved Noble on and strode towards the commotion.

Noble threw the ice-cream van into first and drove away.

Jack peered through the rear window and let out a huge sigh. 'That was too close.'

• • •

When they were far enough away, everyone climbed
out of their hiding places and stretched.

'I thought we were done for,' Slink said.

Obi rubbed his neck. 'I'm never doing that again.
Ever.'

Wren grinned. 'That was fun.'

Charlie's phone beeped. She looked at the display, then at Jack.

'Who's that?' Jack said.

'Hector.'

'Are you nuts?' Jack said. 'You gave him your
number?'

'What does Hector want?' Wren said, shooting
Jack a nasty look.

'He wants to meet us,' Charlie said, reading the
message. 'He says he's found where the actual
Nexus is. Where the government have hidden the
servers.' She looked up at Jack. 'He thinks we can
break into the Nexus directly.'

• • •

A few hours later, Jack was standing by the door
to the bunker, checking his backpack of supplies.

He made sure he had a couple of torches fully charged.

He still didn't trust Hector and wouldn't let him out of his sight, but if Hector was correct – this could be their best chance of getting the virus once and for all.

Charlie, Slink and Wren joined Jack, each with their own bags slung over their shoulders.

'Hector's sent us the coordinates,' Obi called from his chair. 'Relaying them to you, Jack.'

Jack looked at his phone as the map flashed up. 'North London,' he said to the others. According to the GPS it was a place he'd never been to before. He didn't recognise the road name either: Swain's Lane. He looked at the surrounding area. There seemed to be plenty of escape routes should something go wrong. Jack allowed this thought to reassure him a little. 'Let's go,' he said to the others and they marched through the airlock corridor.

• • •

Jack, Charlie, Slink and Wren stood in front of a stone building, two storeys high with a large iron gate in the middle of it and tall leaded windows. It looked strange – somewhere between a church and a castle.

This was the entrance to Highgate West Cemetery.

It was eerily quiet.

'Hector thinks the Nexus is here?' Jack said, dubious.

On either side of the building were brick walls topped with spikes. To the left was a tall metal gate.

'Hey, guys.' Hector strode up the road towards them.

Charlie smiled at him. 'Hi, how are you?'

Hector smiled back. 'I'm good.' He looked at the others. Finally, his eyes rested on Jack. 'All right?'

Jack nodded. 'Hector.'

Slink pointed at the building. 'The Nexus servers are in there?'

'No.' Hector gestured past it. 'Somewhere in the cemetery.'

Jack frowned. 'Are you sure?'

'Definitely.'

'How do you know?' Jack said. It seemed an unlikely place to hide the world's most sophisticated virtual-reality environment.

Hector pulled a netbook from his backpack and

opened it. 'You remember before we left the Nexus access point?'

'I remember you wouldn't listen to me,' Jack said. 'What were you doing?'

'I used Charlie's phone to connect to the computer at my house. Then I ran a tracking program to try and find where the Nexus signal was coming from,' Hector took a breath and looked at Jack, 'but you stopped me before it had time to run a complete trace.'

Jack glanced uneasily at the others. 'Go on.'

'Well, the program had managed to get an IP address.' He pointed at the netbook screen. 'I then wrote a program to search the internet for any records that matched that address.' He glanced around at them all. 'To be honest, I didn't hold out much hope, but then it came up with a result.' He clicked the trackpad and brought up a map of the local area. 'The signal came from here and, after a lot of work, I managed to narrow it down a bit.'

Everyone stood in stunned silence.

Hector glanced at them all again. 'Of course,' he said slowly, 'I can't be sure of the exact location, but I know the signal came from inside the grounds. I can get within ten or so metres of it.' He swallowed.

'That's brilliant,' Charlie said.

Slink nudged Jack's arm and whispered, 'You'll be out of a job soon.'

Jack stiffened and pressed his lips together.

'So,' Hector said, slipping the netbook back into his bag and zipping it up. 'You guys think it's worth a look?'

Slink slapped his hands together. 'This is all me.'

Jack held him back. 'We'll have to make sure no one is around.'

'Hate to break it to you,' Slink said, 'but I think everyone's dead in there.'

Hector smiled. 'He has a point.'

'Fine,' Jack said, letting Slink go. 'Just be careful.'

Slink jogged over to the wall and looked up at the spikes on top. No way over them without being sliced.

Charlie examined the main gate to the side. 'No getting through here either,' she said. 'The padlock is on the inside.'

Jack looked up at the fence. Perhaps if they all put their coats on the spikes, Slink could get over undamaged. Before Jack could suggest this, however, Slink had turned and walked to the main building. 'Where are you going?' Jack said.

'There's a better way.' Slink climbed the building. First he shimmied up the window frames, staying close to the corners, then he wedged his trainers in the gaps of the old stonework and finally hauled himself on to the roof. He ran over the peak and disappeared.

Jack, Charlie, Hector and Wren waited in silence.

After another minute or so, Slink re-emerged. He picked the padlock on the side gate, then swung it open.

The others slipped through.

Jack glanced up and down the road. It was still quiet and it unnerved him. He turned back and hurried after everyone else.

They followed paths flanked by old gravestones covered in weeds and ivy. Moonlight shone through ancient trees, and their branches cast twisted shadows.

'Well done, Hector,' Charlie said. 'You've officially found the creepiest place on planet Earth.'

They flicked on their torches and walked through an arch flanked by Egyptian obelisks.

Beyond was a set of tombs in a large sunken circle, and at the centre of that was a huge cedar tree.

'This place is freakin awesome,' Slink said.

Hector held up a hand, looked at the map on his phone, then gestured to the steps that led down to the circle of tombs. 'It's somewhere there,' he whispered. He pointed to the right and followed the path.

They crept along in silence for a couple more minutes, then Hector found a good vantage point and they sat on the ground, overlooking the circle of tombs.

He glanced at his phone one last time, then pointed at a couple of doorways. 'I'm guessing it's one of those.' He looked at Jack.

Jack didn't like the idea of going down there and trying to break into someone's tomb. Hector had to be wrong, but they didn't have much choice – one of them had to investigate. He was just about to stand when he heard a noise. 'Turn off the torches,' he whispered.

They watched as one of the tomb doors swung open and red light spilled from beyond.

A shadow moved.

Jack stared, holding his breath.

There was a click of a lighter and the face of a man appeared in the glow. He had a scar running down one cheek, and he wore a cap pulled low over his eyes. He looked like a guard of some sort.

The lighter went out, to be replaced by the orange glow of a cigarette.

Jack guessed they had around five minutes. He looked at Charlie. 'We need the exec pen.'

She rummaged in her bag and pulled out a thick silver pen. It had a wireless camera hidden inside it, a transmitter and a battery life that lasted several hours.

Charlie held it out to Jack. 'How are we going to plant it on him?'

Jack took it and looked at Slink. 'Any ideas?'

'I can do it,' Hector whispered, holding out his hand.

Jack hesitated and looked at Charlie.

'Trust him,' she said.

Jack let out a breath and reluctantly handed the pen to Hector.

Hector hurried off into the darkness and they all returned their attention to the tomb and the guard.

Suddenly, Hector appeared on the ledge above him. He glanced down at the man, then pulled back. He silently slipped off his backpack and removed a

254

spool of fine fishing wire. He tied one end of the wire to the pen, lay flat on his stomach and peered down again.

Slowly, Hector fed out the line and the pen dropped towards the guard.

He was aiming to lower the pen into the guard's top jacket pocket. The pen spun on the end of the wire and Hector used his other hand to try to stop it, but the pen continued to rotate.

Jack looked at the guard. A few more puffs on that cigarette and he'd be finished.

Hector lowered the pen some more and it missed the guard's pocket.

Jack swore under his breath.

Hector tried again, but he still couldn't get the pen to slide into the pocket.

The guard turned his head and puffed out a cloud of smoke.

Hector yanked the pen up and out of sight.

Jack judged Hector had one more shot at it.

'What's he doing?' Slink whispered.

Hector was now reeling the line back in.

'He's given up,' Jack said.

Now what were they going to do?

'No,' Wren said. 'Look.'

Hector was unscrewing the end of the pen.

Jack clenched his fists. 'He's going to break it.' He went to stand up but Charlie pulled him back to the ground.

'Watch,' she whispered.

Hector removed the tiny camera and transmitter from the pen. He examined it, and bent out a piece of wire from the back. Hector glanced down at the guard, then shimmied forward, bending over the ledge, his head just a metre or so above the guard's.

Keeping a grip on the brickwork with one hand, Hector reached down to the guard's cap, and with outstretched fingers, eased the camera on to the fabric above the peak.

The guard felt something and looked up, but Hector had leapt back in time and disappeared into the darkness.

The guard stamped out his cigarette and turned on his heels.

Charlie slid a screen with an antenna from her bag and turned it on. They watched from the pen camera's point of view as the man closed the tomb door behind him.

Inside, a red bulb bathed the room in eerie light.

There were three coffins stacked either side of the tomb and a stone plaque on the back wall which had a list of names engraved into it.

The man slid the plaque aside to reveal a keypad behind it. He typed in a six-digit code and leant into the display.

'Biometric,' Charlie whispered. 'There's a camera above the screen and it's scanning his eye.'

There was a second beep and a sliver of white light appeared in the tomb and grew wider as the entire end wall slid aside.

Beyond was a metal landing and a set of steps leading down. Along the ceiling ran thick pipes and halfway down the corridor was a security camera.

The image on the screen flickered.

'It's losing signal,' Charlie said, leaping to her feet. 'We need to get closer.'

The four of them ran around the tombs and met Hector coming in the opposite direction.

'What's wrong?' he whispered.

'Transmission range,' Charlie hissed.

They hurried to the ground above the target tomb and Charlie breathed a sigh of relief as the image came back.

The guard was now walking along a corridor. To his right was a door with a large window next to it. Behind the glass were rows and rows of black server cabinets, each with blinking blue lights like a million fireflies.

The guard continued past the window and reached another door at the end of the hallway. He swiped his card in the lock and entered a room with three monitors on the wall. One displayed a view of outside the tomb, close in on the door. The next one was of a view looking up the corridor from the steps.

The third monitor had a series of temperature readings and in the top-left corner was one word emblazoned in large gold letters –

'Nexus,' Jack said. He looked at Hector. 'You were right.'

In front of the monitors were two chairs and there was another guard sitting in one of them.

He glanced up from his book as the first guard sat down, but he didn't notice the tiny camera on his companion's cap.

Well, not yet at least.

The first guard pulled a phone from his pocket.

Jack leant into the display. The phone didn't have

a signal. The guard started to play a game on his phone.

'So?' Hector whispered to Jack. 'Do you think it's possible to get in there?'

'I have no idea,' Jack said. 'But we have to try.'

CHAPTER TWELVE

BACK AT THE BUNKER, JACK SPENT THE NEXT HOUR
studying the video replay of the guard walking through the Nexus facility. He checked every frame of film for anything they might have missed. Finally satisfied he'd got it all, Jack concentrated on the first target – the camera by the entrance to the tomb. That shouldn't be a problem. Charlie said she had a gadget that could take care of it.

Next, Jack asked Obi to freeze the image on the keypad inside the tomb and he called Charlie over.

'Look at this,' he said, pointing above the keypad where there was a small lens.

'It looks like a standard camera,' Charlie said. 'Probably has Gnome Biometric software running behind it.' She straightened up. 'I'm pretty sure I can get past that. I have an overlay that I can modify that's similar. I need an hour or so. Won't be easy though.'

'Is anything ever easy with us?' Jack said.

'Not so much, no.' Charlie stared at the screen. 'Have you heard from Slink and Hector?'

Jack shook his head. 'It's probably a good sign.'

'Yeah,' Charlie said. 'I guess it means they're not having any trouble getting the stuff they need.' She went to walk away.

'Wait,' Jack said. 'That's not all.'

Obi sped the recording forward until the guard reached the end of the corridor. Obi pressed the Play button. The guard swiped the lock on the door with a card and entered the security room. He sat at the desk with the other guard and started playing with his phone. In the top part of the screen, they could see the three CCTV monitors.

The view of the camera in the hallway panned from side to side, without pausing.

'It's exactly like you thought,' Jack said.

'Good,' Charlie said. 'As long as Slink and Hector sort their end out, I've got the rest covered. We'll need my micro projector.' She turned and hurried down the hallway to her workshop.

Jack looked back to the screens.

'Why couldn't we bring Hector here this time?' Wren said.

'We've been through this,' Jack said, irritated. 'We're not showing him the bunker.'

'But why not?'

Jack went to respond but stopped himself. It was pointless to keep having the same argument with them. 'Now's not a good time,' he said. 'Hector's got a job to do.' He looked at the others but they didn't seem convinced by his response.

'What happens if they get him?' Wren said.

'Who?'

'Del Sarto's henchmen.'

'He's with Slink,' Jack said. 'They'll be fine.'

'But they're after the same thing as us,' Obi said. 'They want the virus too.'

'We don't know that for sure,' Jack said, though Connor and his cronies had been strangely quiet lately. He looked at Obi. 'Send Slink a message, if you want. Warn him to keep an eye out.'

Obi typed a quick message and hit Send.

'Satisfied?' Jack said to Wren.

She crossed her arms.

Jack refocused on the image of the corridor in the

Nexus facility. This was going to be a challenge for Charlie to overcome.

• • •

Later, outside Highgate Cemetery, Slink and Hector were waiting for Jack, Charlie and Wren.

'How was your shopping trip?' Charlie asked them. 'Did you get what you needed?'

Hector grinned. 'No problems.'

'Piece of cake,' Slink said.

'OK,' Jack said. 'This is Charlie's mission.'

Charlie looked at the others. 'Everyone clear on what we have to do?'

They all nodded.

Slink opened the gate and they walked through.

The graveyard was no less creepy the second time around. The sky was cloudy now and, without the moon, the only light came from their torches, which cast strange shadows over ancient stonework, monuments and gravestones.

They reached the ground above the target tomb and Jack and Hector crouched down. Slink lay flat on his stomach in between them and pulled himself over the stone lip, into the circular pathway of tombs. Hector and Jack grabbed his legs, stopping him from falling head first. Slink was now hanging upside down behind the camera trained on the entrance to the tomb.

'Can you see it?' Charlie whispered.

Slink pointed at a crack in the stonework at just the place Jack had worked it out to be. 'It's a wireless camera,' he whispered. 'I can see the antenna.'

Charlie leant over and handed him a small digital camera.

'Can't see how it's getting its power though,' Slink said.

'It doesn't matter.' Charlie pulled a device with two antennae from her bag, put it on the ground and switched it on.

'What's that?' Wren whispered.

'Signal booster.' Charlie opened her netbook and pressed a finger to her ear. 'Obi, are you connected?'

'Yes.'

'Now you should be able to stay in contact with us when we go in.' She opened a window on the netbook and the display divided in two. On the left-hand side was the guard's view from inside the security room. He was still playing a game on his phone, with his feet up on the desk, while the other guard read a book.

Good, neither of them had noticed the camera on his cap.

Slink got the digital pocket camera as close to the CCTV camera as he dared and, watching its angle, pressed the button and took a picture.

He then passed the pocket camera back up to Charlie.

Charlie checked the image against the feed from the guards' room. She shook her head. 'Angle's off.' She passed the camera back to Slink. 'The centre line was OK though,' she whispered. 'Just need to aim it down a fraction.'

'Remind me why we can't just screen grab it from the guards' camera view?' Slink said, grunting and shifting his weight.

'They'd notice a huge drop in the quality of the image,' Charlie said. 'We need a high-res picture to fool them.'

Slink took a breath, raised the camera and took another picture. He handed it back to Charlie and she checked it against the security feed. The two images looked identical.

Charlie quickly hooked up the camera to the net-book and uploaded the image Slink had taken. When it was done, she pulled a black cylinder, five centimetres long, with a button one end, from her pocket and connected it to the spare port on the netbook.

Charlie uploaded the static image and checked it, before finally disconnecting the cylinder again and handing it to Slink. 'Should be good to go.'

Slink jammed the cylinder into the crack in the stonework above the CCTV camera.

He pulled back for a moment.

The cylinder was one of Charlie inventions. It had a powerful transmitter inside that would override the CCTV camera's signal and replace it with the static image she'd just uploaded.

The only problem was that once Slink activated it, there was likely to be a flicker on the guards' monitor.

Slink took a few deep pulls of air, preparing himself. 'Tell me when,' he said.

Everyone watched the display on the netbook.

The first guard was still playing on his phone and the second one was reading his book, but both monitors were clearly in their line of sight.

Charlie went to give Slink the thumbs up but stopped herself. 'Wait.'

The first guard lowered his phone and glanced

over the monitors, then he returned his attention to the game.

'*Now.*'

Slink reached up and flicked the switch on the cylinder. The monitor in front of the guards flickered as it changed images.

Jack held his breath as the first guard's phone lowered.

For several long agonising seconds, he didn't move, then the phone lifted back to his face.

Jack relaxed. Charlie and Slink had done it.

The image on the guards' monitor was now just a static picture.

Jack and Hector hauled Slink back above the tomb and stood up.

'Phase one, complete,' Charlie said, handing Jack the netbook. 'Now for the next part.' She looked at the others. 'Let's get in position.'

They walked to the edge of the circular path. Jack, Slink and Hector made their way to the centre circle of grass under the cedar tree and lay down on their stomachs opposite the tomb, while Wren and Charlie went right and disappeared into the darkness.

Jack watched the netbook display of the guard's view. Now would be a perfect time for him to come outside for a cigarette, but that was hoping for too much.

The seconds dragged like minutes, the minutes like hours, and still the guard didn't move.

Maybe he wasn't a heavy smoker. Perhaps he'd only just had a cigarette. Or maybe he wasn't going to have another?

Twenty minutes later, the guard stood up and walked to the door.

'We're up,' Jack whispered into his microphone. His pulse quickened. They only had one shot at this. *One* shot. It had to run perfectly.

He looked up as the guard emerged from the tomb, glanced around, then pulled a lighter from his pocket and lit a cigarette.

'Obi,' Jack whispered into his mic. 'Bring up the other cameras.'

Two more views appeared on the netbook's screen. One was from Wren's shoulder cam and the other was from Charlie's.

'Go, Wren,' Charlie whispered.

Wren circled the tombs and, keeping low, crept around the corner, just far enough to see the guard.

She scooped up a stone from the ground and tossed it at the tomb door.

The guard spun, grabbed his torch, flicked it on and shone it in Wren's direction, but she kept back in the shadows.

The beam of the guard's torch swept from left to right.

Wren grabbed another stone and threw it.

The guard's eyes snapped in that direction and he took several steps away from the door, searching for the source of the noise.

Charlie sneaked silently around the corner and darted into the tomb behind him.

Wren stayed back, still hidden, out of reach of the guard's torch as he continued to look around.

Jack watched the view from Charlie's shoulder cam as she hurried over to the keypad and pulled an exact replica of the keypad and camera she'd made. The only difference was her device was a fraction bigger.

Charlie clipped the fake keypad over the top of the original and switched it on. It glowed blue and, as far as Jack could tell, there was no way you'd easily spot the difference.

Charlie then pulled a smartphone out of her pocket and checked the screen. 'No way,' she muttered.

'What?' Jack said.

'The camera on the modified keyboard isn't working.'

Obi brought up a new pop-up box on the netbook and, sure enough, it showed a black square where the image was supposed to be.

Charlie stepped forward and switched the overlay device on and off again.

From Wren's camera view, the guard had now given up the search and was walking away from her, back towards the tomb's entrance.

Jack swore. 'Charlie,' he whispered. 'The guard's coming.'

'I'm going as fast as I can,' she hissed. Charlie tapped the side of the overlay but the camera image stayed black. 'Stupid thing.' Charlie lifted it off and checked the wires on the back. 'It was working. I checked it like a million times.'

Jack looked to his left. The guard was coming around the corner. 'Not enough time, Charlie,' he whispered into the mic. 'Get out of there.'

'Wait, I've almost got it.' Charlie pushed a wire and the camera sprang to life.

Jack could now see the image on the netbook screen.

Charlie quickly slid the device back over the keypad and grabbed her bag from the floor.

The guard's torch beam bounced off the tomb door and Jack knew Charlie wouldn't be able to get out unseen.

Charlie had obviously realised this too because she was turning on the spot, searching for somewhere to hide.

There were three coffins stacked on top of each other on the right and the same on the left. They were pushed right up against the wall so there was nowhere for her to hide behind them.

Suddenly, Hector sprang to his feet and ran off.

'Great,' Jack whispered. 'He's just abandoned us.'

Charlie squatted down in the corner of the tomb and switched off her torch, but it wouldn't be enough. The guard would easily spot her. The best she could do was try to make a break for it.

Jack cocked his head to the side and was about to tell her to get out of there when there was a snapping sound.

Jack froze.

So did the guard. He shone his torch at the cedar tree.

Jack didn't waste a second. 'Get out of there, Charlie,' he breathed.

There was another snapping sound – this time further away – and the beam of the guard's torch moved in the direction of the noise.

Charlie peered around the door, then silently slipped out and ran the opposite way to the guard.

From the guard's camera view, Jack watched as he stepped inside the tomb and closed the door behind him.

Hector reappeared.

'That was you?' Jack said.

He nodded.

'Thanks.'

'No problem.'

The guard typed in the six-digit security code and leant into the camera. His eye filled the window on the netbook display.

There was a short pause, then the LED turned green.

The door slid aside and the guard walked down the steps.

A minute later, Jack, Charlie, Hector, Slink and Wren were standing outside the door to the tomb.

'Obi, keep us updated,' Charlie whispered into her headset.

'Will do. The guard is back in the room with the other one. All is quiet.'

Charlie opened the door to the tomb and they went inside.

She unclipped the overlay device she'd made and connected it to her smartphone. 'I'm checking the code he typed first. It's seven, seven, three, five, nine, two.'

Jack typed in the numbers.

Now for the really clever part.

The camera in the overlay had captured an image of the guard's eye. Charlie brought it up on her smartphone and held it in front of the keypad.

The LED changed to green and the door slid open.

'Hurry,' Charlie said to the others, and they stepped on to the metal landing. She pointed up at the camera. It was panning from left to right, but didn't reach the part they were standing on.

Because the camera was moving, they couldn't fix it with a static image and an alarm would sound if they tampered with the camera's cables. So, Charlie had come up with a unique idea to solve the problem.

She looked at Slink. 'All yours.'

Slink stepped on to the handrail and pulled himself up, using the pipes that ran along the ceiling. Hanging upside down, with his arms wrapped around the pipes in a bear hug, he inched his way along.

Jack kept an eye on the guards' door at the end of the corridor.

Slink's feet slipped and he hung by just his hands.

One foot swung past the front of the camera.

'I saw that on their monitor,' Obi said.

Charlie flinched. 'Did the guards?'

'No.'

Jack shook his head.

Charlie looked pale.

Slink regained his grip and pulled his feet back up. He shimmied along the pipes, then pushed open a ceiling panel. With a quick glance down at the others, he hauled himself inside and vanished.

After several seconds, he reappeared and gave them the OK signal: he'd found and severed the phone line, along with the main alarm. Now there was no way the guards could call for help.

Slink lowered himself back to the pipes and continued to shimmy along them until he was directly above the camera mounted on the wall.

275

Jack, Hector and Wren stayed back as Charlie reached into her bag and pulled out a telescopic rod. She extended it out to a metre or so and clipped a modified camera and projector to the end of it.

While she checked it was on and working, Jack motioned for Hector to get ready. 'You're up.'

Hector slipped off his backpack and removed his hoodie, revealing a long-sleeved white shirt underneath.

Next, he took off his shoes and jeans. Beneath them he was wearing white jogging bottoms tucked into white socks. He pulled a pair of white gloves from his pocket and put them on too.

Charlie stepped up on to the handrail and extended the device on the rod out to Slink.

Slink reached, but couldn't quite grab it. He shifted his weight, held on by one hand and tried again, but still couldn't grasp it.

Jack motioned for Charlie to step down. He unclipped the device from the rod, looked up at Slink and mouthed, 'Ready?'

Slink nodded.

In one fluid movement, Jack tossed it up to him and Slink deftly caught it with his free hand.

Jack turned and smiled at Charlie.

She cocked an eyebrow at him.

Slink clipped the modified device to the bracket directly above the CCTV camera.

Charlie held up her smartphone and checked the display. The modified camera showed the exact same view of the corridor as the CCTV camera. Also, as it panned slowly left and right, the custom camera followed. They looked identical.

Charlie recorded the video as it moved back and forth a few times, then looked at Hector. 'Ready.' She handed him a swipe card with a circuit board on the back and a transmitter.

Hector slipped them into his pocket and pulled on a white balaclava. He was now dressed in white head-to-toe, like a strange negative image of a ninja. Except for his eyes, not a single part of him showed.

Charlie pressed a button on her smartphone and the tiny projector above the camera came on. It transmitted a recorded image of the hallway and she adjusted it until it perfectly overlaid the real thing.

'Looks aligned,' Charlie said to Hector.

Wren frowned. 'I don't get it. What's the point of that?'

'Watch,' Charlie said.

Hector reached the bottom of the stairs and, keeping his face to the wall, edged down the corridor.

The CCTV camera swung in his direction and the image of the hallway was projected on to his body.

Hector's white clothes acted like a projector screen. From Jack's vantage point, he could see Hector clearly, because the image didn't line up, but from the guard's point of view, Hector was invisible.

'Can't see him on the guard's monitor,' Obi said. 'It's brilliant, Charlie.'

Charlie grinned.

She'd made the micro projector device a year back, and had been itching to try it out ever since.

Jack kept looking between the CCTV camera and to Hector edging up the corridor.

Each step was slow and precise.

And each second stretched to eternity.

Jack, Charlie, Slink and Wren waited, keeping as still as statues, hardly daring to breath.

Finally, Hector made it to the end of the corridor and turned to face the door. He pulled Charlie's swipe card with the circuit board from his pocket and silently slipped it into the lock on the door.

He stepped aside and waved his hand up and down.

Charlie connected her phone via Bluetooth to the card. She pressed a few buttons and there was a click from the lock. 'Got it,' she said. 'They ain't getting out of there.' She turned to the others. 'Come on.'

They hurried down the steps.

Hector pulled off his balaclava and knocked on the door. 'All right in there?'

'What are you doing, you idiot?' Jack said, storming over to him.

The lock rattled and there were muffled shouts and banging.

Jack threw his arms up. 'Great, now they know we're here.'

'Why does it matter?' Hector said.

'Because the guards might have sat there for ages,' Jack said, annoyed. 'It was clean. Now they know we're here and will try everything to get out.' He shot Hector a contemptuous look and marched to the server room door. He opened it and gestured them all inside.

They now stood in front of the rows of server cabinets.

'Nexus,' Hector breathed, his eyes wide. He glanced at Jack. 'I wish I had time to see it.'

Jack strode over to the main terminal. He reached into his pocket and pulled out a USB drive. 'I'll transfer the virus to this.'

'Is that the same program you used to put the virus into Proteus's servers?' Hector asked.

Jack hesitated.

'What's wrong?' Hector said.

Jack shook himself. 'Nothing.'

Hector turned to the server cabinets.

Jack reached into his pocket, pulled out another USB pen stick and slid it into one of the sockets.

He took a breath and set to work. He typed a quick program, checked the code, and straightened up. A progress bar moved quickly, filling up with red. 'We'll have the virus in less than a minute.' He turned around.

Hector was frowning at the server cabinets.

Charlie noticed him. 'Are you OK?'

'I've been thinking,' Hector said. 'I bet they've copied the virus already.' He glanced at the monitor and the progress bar, then back to the server cabinets. 'That's what I would do if it was me. You know, just in case the virus escaped or something. I'd make sure there was a backup.'

'How do you think they've done it?' Charlie said.

Hector pointed to a cluster of cabinets at the back of the room. 'Look at the connections. Those look like backup servers. I reckon they've taken a clone of the Nexus, which will include the virus's program. We need to destroy them.'

Charlie looked at Jack. 'He has a point.'

Jack stared at Hector and didn't respond.

'First, we need to pull out the wires from the backup Nexus to the main Nexus,' Hector said. 'Then we can wipe the hard drives and destroy the copy.'

'Ok,' Jack said, eyeing him. 'Let's see what happens.'

Charlie hurried over to the cabinets. 'Open them all,' she said.

Jack, Slink and Wren opened the front of the cabinets and Charlie started disconnecting wires.

The main door slammed shut.

'No,' Slink shouted. He ran to the door and tried the handle. 'It's locked.'

Understanding what had just happened, Jack casually walked between the cabinets and looked through the window. As he'd expected, he couldn't see any guards but on the window ledge was a chewing gum wrapper folded into the shape of a crow.

Hector stepped into view, on the other side of the glass, and held up a USB drive. He waved it back and forth.

'What are you doing?' Slink shouted.

Jack glanced at the computer terminal, but he needn't have bothered, he knew it was his drive. In its place was a blue one. Obviously, Hector had replaced it.

Jack didn't bother to grab the blue drive from the USB port. Hector's program would have infected the system already.

Jack's gaze moved back to the window.

Hector adjusted his headset. 'Well, well,' he said in a smug tone. 'You're all as stupid as I thought you were.' He moved close to the glass. 'I've won . . . *I've won*. You hear that, Jack?' Hector straightened up and continued, 'I suppose you're wondering what's happened to you?'

'Not really,' Jack said.

Hector's eyes flickered. 'Now, now, Jack. No need to be rude. No one likes a sore loser. I'm sure the others want to understand what's going on.' He looked at Charlie, Slink and Wren. 'Right?'

None of them responded.

Hector paced back and forth in front of the

window. 'My real name is Quentin Del Sarto.' He paused, as if letting that piece of news sink in.

Charlie looked at Jack. 'Del Sarto.'

'I'm glad you recognise the name.' Hector's lip curled and his voice was full of venom. 'Benito del Sarto is my father.'

'*Is*?' Slink said. 'You mean he's still alive?'

Hector's cold eyes moved to Slink, then back to Jack. 'You almost killed him in that theatre. You left him for dead. The fire.' Hector took a breath, seeming to compose himself. 'My father is in a coma. He has third degree burns over eighty per cent of his body.'

'He did that himself,' Wren said.

Hector shot her a nasty look. 'Shut your mouth.'

'Hey,' Slink said, stepping in front of Wren. 'When I get hold of you, I'm gonna –'

'You couldn't do a thing to me,' Hector snarled.

'Oh, yeah?' Slink moved to the window. 'Open the door and find out.'

Hector laughed at him. 'Pathetic.' He looked at the others. 'Now I have the virus, I'm going to finish what my dad started. I'm going to find this bunker of yours and destroy it. Then I'm going to expose your little gang to the rest of the world.' He smiled. 'Consider this payback.'

Hector spun on his heels and marched up the steps.

An alarm sounded.

CHAPTER THIRTEEN

SLINK SHOUTED ABOVE THE ALARM, 'I THOUGHT I got that?'

'You did.' Jack rushed over to the computer terminal. He typed a few commands and the alarm stopped, but the damage was done. The police would be on their way.

'Jack, I've been thinking.' Slink leant against the wall and crossed his arms. 'I've changed my mind. I'm not sure we should let Hector join the Urban Outlaws.'

'Me neither,' Wren said.

'That goes for me too,' Obi said in their ears.

Charlie was still staring through the window. 'He tricked us.' She looked at Jack. 'He tricked us, Jack. How did that happen?'

The fans in the server cabinets started to speed up.

'What now?' she said.

Jack checked the computer terminal. 'Payback is right,' he muttered.

Knowing they'd disabled the main building's alarm, Hector had infected the servers, triggering their internal alarms. He'd also planted his own program and it was now overheating the processors. Hector's plan was either to burn the Outlaws to a crisp in there – like Del Sarto senior – or, if they survived that, the police would turn up and arrest them.

Either way, Hector had planned this moment carefully.

Charlie examined the door, but there was no way to open it from the inside.

Slink looked up at the ceiling. 'There has to be a way out of here.' But his eyes gave away that he knew as well as Jack did. They were trapped.

The ceiling was solid plaster and it had no panels, hatches, or air vents big enough for Slink to crawl into.

'Hector's got the virus,' Wren said to Jack, her eyes wide and panicked. 'We have to stop him.'

Jack held up a USB stick. 'No he doesn't.' He yanked out Hector's drive, threw it across the room, plugged in his own USB stick with the program on it and started the transfer. In a minute or so, the virus would be on Jack's drive as originally planned.

'What? Wait a sec,' Charlie said. 'Hector *hasn't* got the virus?'

Jack shook his head.

Charlie pointed at the terminal. 'It's still on there?'

Jack nodded.

Charlie put her hands on her hips. 'OK. How long have you known?'

'Known what?' Jack said with an air of innocence.

'How long have you known that Hector was going to stitch us up? That he wasn't who he said he was?'

'That he's a lying worm,' Slink added.

'I didn't know for certain,' Jack said. 'Well, not until about five minutes ago. It was then that I guessed something wasn't right.'

'Guessed something wasn't right?' Charlie repeated, her voice raising an octave. 'When? What?'

'It was just before I plugged in my drive,' Jack said. 'Hector asked me if I was going to use the program I'd used to attract the virus on to Proteus's servers.'

Charlie nodded. 'Yeah. I remember. Hector already knows about Proteus and the program. So what?'

'You're right – he does know the government computer was called Proteus,' Jack said, glancing at Wren and Slink. 'And Hector also knows I wrote a program to attract the virus. Which is why it took me a second to realise what was wrong with what he said.'

Wren's eyebrows pulled together. 'What was wrong then?'

'The only way he could've known that I'd used the program to attract the virus to Proteus's servers in the first place was if Connor, Monday or Cloud had told him. Apart from us, they were the only ones there at the time.'

Charlie squeezed her eyes shut. 'I used Cloud's laptop when we were at Proteus.' She opened her eyes and stared at Jack. 'That's how they knew. It's all my fault.'

'No, it isn't. I asked you to use Cloud's laptop that day.' Jack sighed and leant against the desk. 'It's all starting to make sense. The way the agents turned up at Hector's apartment, forcing us to take him with us. And the same after the Science Museum.'

Wren folded her arms. 'If all this is true, then why didn't you tell us? Why let Hector escape?'

'It was a little difficult to say anything with him standing right there,' Jack said. 'Anyway, I wanted to see what he was going to do. And, I wanted him to think he had the virus.'

'You still could've told us.'

'No, I couldn't.'

'Yes,' Wren said. '*You could*. We're a team. We could've helped.'

'I would have punched his lights out,' Slink said.

Jack's eyebrows rose. 'Even if I had managed to tell you Hector was a traitor, would you have believed me?'

'Yes,' Wren said, looking at Charlie and Slink for support.

They both nodded.

'Oh, come on,' Jack said, 'You've been hassling me to make Hector one of the Urban Outlaws. If I had suggested, even hinted that he was up to something, you would've –'

'All right, all right,' Charlie said. The sound of the fans was growing louder and more intense. 'We can argue about this later.' She took a breath. 'So, how are we getting out of here?'

'I have a plan.' Jack checked the monitor. The

virus had transferred to his drive. He unplugged it and slipped it into his pocket.

How long did they have left before the police arrived? Before Highgate Cemetery was flooded with armed agents?

Jack looked at Charlie. 'When I say, I need you to release the lock on the guards' door. OK?'

'What?' she said, unbelieving. 'Have you lost your mind?'

'It's the only way to get out of here quickly.'

'Yeah?' Slink said. 'Quick, maybe, but they'll put us in prison, Jack.'

'Do you have a better idea?'

Slink glanced around the room and his shoulders slumped. 'No.'

Jack turned away from him. 'Charlie?'

'Are you sure you want me to release the lock?' she said.

'Yes, but give me a minute, OK?' Jack had a plan, but between the moment he'd realised Hector was up to something and now, he hadn't had enough time to think it through entirely or consider any alternatives. It was this or nothing.

Jack quickly gave Charlie, Slink and Wren their instructions, spelling out exactly what they had to do.

When he had finished, they looked puzzled, but nodded their agreement.

'Positions,' Jack said. 'And make sure your faces are covered.'

They pulled up their bandanas and hoods.

Wren hurried between the server cabinets and disappeared.

Slink climbed on top of a cabinet near the door and braced himself above it, in the corner where the walls met, keeping out of sight.

Charlie pulled her custom stun gun from her bag and laid it on the floor behind the door. She straightened up and looked at Jack. 'You do realise this probably won't work, don't you?'

Jack shrugged. 'It's the best I've got right now.' He stepped to the window. 'OK, disengage the lock.'

Charlie typed in to her phone and Jack watched the light on the guards' door turn from red to green.

In less than a second, the door flew open and the men, guns drawn, burst into the hallway. Their eyes locked on to Jack and Charlie through the glass and for a long while no one moved.

Jack wondered if the guards were considering leaving them in there until backup arrived.

The lead guard frowned through the window over Jack's shoulder. This seemed to snap the man to his senses and he moved to the door.

Gun still raised and ready, he unlocked the door, opened it and stepped inside. 'Hands up.'

Jack and Charlie did as they were told and raised their hands high into the air.

The lead guard glanced at the servers, then back to Jack and Charlie. 'What have you done?'

Neither of them answered.

'Get out of there,' the lead guard said. '*Now*.' He waved his gun and stepped back.

Slowly, hands still raised, Jack and Charlie walked past him and into the hallway.

The other guard shouted, 'Look.' He waved his gun at the window.

'What?' the lead guard said.

'There's another kid in there.'

They both stared as Wren darted from one server cabinet and hid behind another.

'It's just a little one,' the lead guard said. 'Go get her.'

The other guard stepped to the door and hesitated.

'What's wrong with you? Get going.'

He turned back. 'I don't want to shoot a kid.'

'You don't need to. Just threaten her a little. She'll come out of there all nice and quiet like.'

The other guard entered the room, his gun lowered but ready.

Suddenly, the door slammed shut behind him and there was a muffled cry.

'Hey,' the lead guard shouted. 'What are you doing?'

No one answered.

The lead guard kept his gun trained on Jack and Charlie as he edged to the window and peered through. Obviously seeing nothing, he stepped to the door and grabbed the handle.

He suddenly went rigid and his whole body convulsed.

Jack and Charlie ducked as the gun swung wildly around in his hand.

'Slink,' Jack shouted. 'Enough.'

The guard let go of the door handle and fell to his knees, his eyes glazed.

Charlie kicked the pistol out of his hand and it skidded along the floor out of reach.

The door opened.

Slink held the stun gun and looked down at it. 'I have got to get me one of these.'

Jack took it from him.

Inside the server room, the other guard lay on the floor, moaning.

'Think I broke his collar bone when I landed on him.' Slink touched the guard's shoulder and he yelled in pain. 'Yep, definitely broken.'

'Where's his gun?' Jack said.

Slink pointed under a server cabinet as Wren ran up to them.

'Er, guys?' It was Obi.

Jack answered, 'Yeah?'

'There's a load of cars heading your way.'

'By a "load",' Jack said, 'how many do you mean exactly?'

'Five. Oh, wait, *six*.'

'Police?'

'Worse.'

Jack glanced at Charlie. 'Agents?'

'Yep,' Obi said.

'How far out?'

'I reckon you've got about five minutes.'

'Let's get out of here.' Jack hurried over to Slink and they both helped the injured guard to his feet.

Wren and Charlie lifted the other electrocuted guard up too and they struggled up the stairs with him.

Jack glanced back at the server room.

At the top they walked along the landing and into the tomb. Charlie quickly removed the keypad overlay and they stepped out into the darkness.

They sat the guards down on the stone steps that led back out.

The main guard scowled at them. 'You're going to get into a lot of trouble for this.'

Slink grinned at him. 'Not today, cupcake.'

They heard sirens approaching in the distance.

'Time to go,' Charlie said.

They all started to jog away, but Jack turned back to the tomb and hesitated.

'Jack,' Charlie hissed. 'Come on. Hurry.'

Jack handed her the USB drive with the virus on it.

Charlie looked shocked. 'What are you up to?'

Jack addressed the entire group. 'Get away from here. Go – as quick as you can.'

'Why?' Wren said. 'What are you doing?'

Jack ignored her question. 'Get to the bunker. Let me know when you're safe.' Without looking back, he marched to the tomb.

When he reached the entrance, Jack glanced over his shoulder to make sure the others had gone, and he hurried inside. He jogged down the steps, along the corridor and into the server room.

The fans were still running high, but the servers seemed to be holding up so far.

That wouldn't last for much longer – Hector's program was obviously targeting the hardware itself.

He could not let the Nexus be destroyed. It was the world's most sophisticated virtual reality and it wasn't owned by criminals – it was government property. Jack wasn't a supporter of the government, but if he allowed another one of their advanced computer systems to be wrecked, the Outlaws would be forever hunted. The government would constantly be on their backs.

Besides, who knew how many lives the Nexus could possibly save by running those anti-terrorist simulations?

No, Jack had to try to stop Hector's program, before it did too much damage.

He sat in front of the terminal and set to work. Jack opened up a command box and typed. Hector's program was clever – the way it infected the system and sped up the fans. Hector had realised that the Urban Outlaws would shut down all the alarm systems and telephone lines to the building, but Jack had over-looked something – the maintenance alarms on the servers themselves. Right now, they were sending out a signal to say they were in trouble.

He opened several more terminal boxes and started searching for the main program, but he couldn't find it anywhere. He looked in several obvious places for the file and even in the redundant folders, but it was nowhere.

Where was it?

'Jack?' Obi said in his ear.

'What?' Jack opened another command prompt and tried a new search.

'The agents are in front of the main gates. They're getting out of their cars and they're on their way to you.'

'What about the others?'

'They got away. They're safe.'

Jack let out a breath. That only left a few minutes for the agents to get through the graveyard and to the Nexus.

Jack stared at the screen. It made no sense – Hector's program was software, which meant it –

Jack's thoughts froze.

'That's it.'

He quickly opened another box and searched – he found the code and it wasn't a full program, not as such – it was just a few simple commands. Jack's eyes went wide.

He heard the agents rushing into the tomb and along the metal landing.

Jack swore. Hector's program was designed to speed the server fans up. That was all. It didn't attack the hardware. It had no chance of destroying the Nexus. It was another one of Hector's stupid tricks.

There were footfalls on the stairs.

Jack deactivated Hector's program and the fans slowed.

Several agents ran into the room, guns aimed at him.

'Get away from that.' A tall agent stepped forward, grabbed Jack by his shirt and pulled him from the chair.

Jack hit the floor and looked up at the screen.

Hector had tricked him again.

He ground his teeth.

The tall agent stood over Jack, his face twisted into rage. 'You're in a whole heap of trouble, kid.' He grabbed Jack by the collar and dragged him from the room.

Back outside the main gates, the agents handcuffed Jack and bundled him into the back of a car.

He sat there and watched as agents and cars flooded the road. A van turned up and four techies carrying toolboxes were escorted inside.

Several agents stood in a group and seemed to be in an animated discussion. They were probably wondering how a kid had broken into one of their most secure facilities.

Two break-ins in the last couple of weeks was probably making them re-evaluate their security.

It was at that point Jack wondered if the agents would link him and the others to the Winchester Theatre they'd destroyed.

He hoped not.

If they did, he'd probably be locked up for the rest of his life.

Jack glanced at the doors in the back of the car – there were no locks or handles on the inside.

His hands were cuffed behind his back and the agents had removed his phone, headset and everything he had in his pockets.

Jack lowered his head, closed his eyes and wondered what they were going to do with him. Where would they take him? A secret prison? Interrogation? Would they torture a fifteen-year-old boy?

The driver's door opened and someone got in.

Jack looked up and gasped. '*Slink*,' he said, glancing at the agents. They weren't looking in their direction. 'What are you doing here?'

Slink grinned and put a finger to his lips. He looked at the keys in the ignition.

'No,' Jack said. 'Don't even think about it.'

'It's the quickest way.'

'Not if we don't want to be seen.' Jack glanced through the rear window. Slink would have to reverse between three parked cars and turn around in a narrow driveway before they could escape. Jack looked forward again and tried to keep his voice casual. 'You don't know how to drive.'

'I've seen it done though.'

'Please, Slink, just get me out of here. OK?'

Slink let out an annoyed breath. 'Fine.' He hit a button on the dash to unlock the doors and they clunked.

Jack looked through the windscreen, but the agents hadn't heard – they were still talking.

Slink yanked the keys out of the ignition and examined them. 'The key for the handcuffs isn't on here.'

'The agents must have it.'

'Shall I get Wren and see if she can –'

'No,' Jack said. 'Let's just get out of here.'

Slink quietly slipped out of the car and opened the rear-passenger door.

Keeping his head low, Jack shimmied along the seat and got out.

Slink bent down by the rear car tyre.

'What are you doing?' Jack whispered.

Slink unscrewed the dust cap and jammed a small stone in the air valve. It hissed.

Slink was about to do the same to the next car when an agent shouted, 'Oi.'

The other agents turned and spotted Slink and Jack.

'Go,' Jack shouted and, with his hands still cuffed behind his back, they ran down the road – the agents close behind.

'Charlie,' Slink yelled into his headset. 'The plan needs a slight tweak.'

Suddenly, she shot from the trees like a bullet. Charlie was wearing her Rollerblades and she sped past Jack and Slink.

Jack glanced back and watched as she rammed into the first agent. He hit the road, hard, and another agent tripped over him.

A third agent leapt clear and shouted. He went to

grab a pistol from his belt but Charlie jabbed the stun gun into his back.

The agent yelled in pain and tumbled forward.

More agents ran from the main gate and headed straight for them.

Charlie sped off down the road and disappeared around the corner.

'Come on,' Slink shouted, and pulled Jack through a side gate.

They ran into a smaller graveyard and Slink helped Jack over a low wall. 'Wait,' he said, and they stayed close to the wall, hidden.

A few minutes later, Charlie joined them. 'They're coming this way,' she whispered. She handed Slink the wallet of picks and quickly took off her Rollerblades and slid them into her bag.

Slink tried to pick the lock on Jack's handcuffs. 'I can't do it,' he whispered.

'Give them here,' Charlie said.

In a few seconds, the handcuffs sprang open.

Jack rubbed his wrists and peered over the wall. He caught a glimpse of one agent searching between the gravestones.

He glanced around, then beckoned for Slink's headset.

Slink handed it to him.

Jack slipped it on and whispered, 'Obi?'

'Here.'

'Bring up a satellite map of the area. Guide us home, but keep us away from the main roads and security cameras.'

The three of them stood and followed Obi's instructions, through back gardens, down the side of houses and along winding paths.

After an hour of this, they reached the nearest Tube station and Jack finally allowed himself to relax.

• • •

Back at the bunker, sitting at the dining table for a debrief, Jack explained how Hector had tricked him with the Nexus servers.

Charlie nodded thoughtfully. 'He had us all fooled, Jack. You're the only one who saw through him.'

Jack was about to answer when Obi called him over.

'You'd better come and look at this. It's a private message to you with a video file attached.'

Jack stood up and strode over to him.

Obi pointed at the screen.

It was an image of Hector and he looked angry.

'Where's this from?' Jack said.

'Cerberus forum.'

Everyone gathered around Obi's chair.

Jack took a breath. Somehow, he knew Hector hadn't sent him a 'Congratulations for tricking me' video message. 'OK,' he said, bracing himself. 'Let's see.'

Obi pressed Play.

'I have your friend,' Hector said in a cold, flat tone. The camera panned round to reveal Noble with his hands and legs tied to a chair. His face was bruised, his lip bloody and his clothes were torn. Connor and Monday stood either side of him, arms crossed.

'No,' Charlie breathed.

Jack felt his chest tighten and the world drop.

The view moved back to Hector. 'So, as you can see, I'm in control.' He leant into the camera. 'Bring the virus to the Shard.' He moved closer, his eyes filling the entire screen. 'No tricks, Jack, I mean it. I want to see all five of you standing in front of me. I'll know if you try to fool me again.' He paused, as if he could see through the camera and into Jack's eyes. Finally, he leant back. 'One hour.' Hector glanced in Noble's direction. 'I'd advise you not to be late.'

The display went dark.

Jack stared at the screen. *An hour?* That wasn't enough time. He glanced at the others. They looked pale.

'Why does he want us to meet him at the Shard?' Wren said.

'Yeah,' Obi said. 'That makes no sense. Why somewhere so public?'

'No one will be there at this time of night,' Charlie said.

Jack stepped back. 'He knows there's limited ways in and out of the place.'

'Jack?' Charlie said, her voice quiet.

He looked at her.

'You've got a plan, right?'

Jack's eyes moved to the clock on the screen. He had ten minutes to spare. He grabbed one of Obi's keyboards and started to type.

CHAPTER FOURTEEN

AN HOUR LATER, JACK AND THE OTHERS WERE standing in the lift of the Shard. It was the tallest building in London: a huge spike of glass pointing straight into the sky.

They kept their hoods up, their bandanas over their mouths and noses. Accompanying them were two beefy men wearing grey suits. Each had an unmistakable bulge under their jackets – a good indication they were armed.

Where did the Del Sarto family find these henchmen? Was there a company you called or something? A hotline?

Jack watched the floor numbers on the display increase. He hated heights, but Slink had wanted to climb the Shard ever since it was completed and had been disappointed when some protestors beat him to it.

The lift stopped at the thirty-third floor and Hector's minders motioned for the five of them to step out.

'Why are we getting off here?' Charlie said in Jack's ear.

'It's as far as it goes,' Jack whispered back. 'We have to get in another lift to go higher.' A prospect that made Jack's stomach do a backflip.

One of the men grabbed Jack's shoulder. 'Stop the chatter.' And together they marched around the corner, where another man was waiting for them.

This guy wasn't so low-key. He held a rifle across his chest, ready.

Hector's minders pushed the five of them against the wall and patted them down. Next, one of the men waved a grey wand over their clothes, checking for metal objects.

Finally, he stepped back. 'They're clean.'

The men ushered Jack and the others into the next lift and they went up to floor sixty-eight.

When they finally stepped out, they were greeted by a wall of glass. This was the Shard's covered viewing deck and the cityscape before them was spectacular. Millions of lights sparkled in the darkness and a slight orange haze hung over the landscape.

Jack stepped back and tried to remember if he'd told Hector he got vertigo. *Was that why Hector had insisted they meet here?* To intimidate him? Jack balled his fists and refused to show any fear.

'Go.' One of the men nudged Jack and the others around the corner to a flight of stairs leading up.

When they reached the top, they found themselves in the upper viewing deck. It had no roof and the wind whistled over the tops of the glass walls.

To the left stood Connor, Cloud, Monday and Hector.

Behind them was Noble. His hands were tied behind his back, his face bloodied and bruised.

Jack lowered his hood and bandana. 'Are you OK?'

'He's fine,' Connor said, stepping in front of Noble.

'I wasn't asking you,' Jack said in a level tone. He looked at Noble.

'No lasting damage,' Noble said. 'I'll live.'

'Don't be so sure about that,' Connor snarled. He looked as though he'd like to kill them all right there and then.

Jack ignored him and kept his gaze on Noble. 'I'm sorry,' he said.

'It's not your fault.'

'As touching as this is,' Hector said, 'we have work

309

to do.' He addressed one of his men. 'Did you frisk them?'

The man nodded. 'Yes. Unarmed.'

'Phones? Radios? Any kind of hidden trans-mitters?'

He shook his head. 'No communication devices.'

'Good. Wait downstairs.' As the three minders left, Hector looked at Jack. 'Playing by the rules for once,' he said. 'That must be killing you.' He glanced at the others – they still had their hoods and bandanas up. 'Camera shy?' he asked. 'There really is no point.'

None of them responded.

Hector held out his hand to Jack. 'The virus.'

Jack fished in his pocket and pulled out the USB drive.

Hector snatched it from him and handed it to Cloud. 'Check it.'

Cloud knelt down, unzipped her bag and pulled out a laptop. She plugged the USB drive in and set to work.

'Why so quiet, Jack?' Hector said.

Jack kept his eyes on Cloud.

'*Jack*,' Hector shouted. 'Answer me.'

Jack looked at him. 'What do you want me to say?'

'That I've beaten you. That I'm the better hacker. I'm better than you.' Hector's eyes burned with intensity. 'Admit it,' he said through gritted teeth. 'What's it like to be outsmarted, Jack? I bet it burns you up, huh?'

'It's the virus,' Cloud said finally.

'Use the modified modem, transfer the virus directly to my server. And make sure it can't escape.'

Cloud plugged in the modem. 'Transfer started.' She looked up. 'Sixty seconds and it should be done.'

Hector eyed Jack. 'Well,' he said. 'Now we have to deal with you and your –' he glanced at the others – '*gang.*'

Connor took a step forward. 'That's easily taken care of.'

Hector kept his gaze on Jack and he smirked. 'How would you do it?'

'I'll throw them over that.' Connor pointed at the lowest part of the glass wall.

'How high up are we?' Hector said, as if he were genuinely interested.

'Two hundred and forty-four metres,' Connor said. 'Give or take.'

Hector's eyebrows rose. 'That would make quite a mess. Perhaps you could just put them in sealed bags and drop them into the Thames.'

'What are you going to do with the virus?' Wren said.

'What am I going to do with it?' Hector regarded her for a moment. 'I'm going to finish what my dad started before you put him into a coma.' He stepped towards Wren and his lip curled into a snarl. 'After I've had you all killed, I'm going to steal every top-secret document I can, and sell them to the highest bidders.'

'You're crazy,' Wren said.

'No,' Hector said in a low voice. 'I'm at the beginning of a new era in the world's history.' He reached for Wren, but she flinched away from him.

'The transfer is complete.' Cloud closed the laptop, slid it back into her bag, stood up and handed Hector's phone back to him.

'Good. Well done.' Hector gestured. 'Time to go.'

'You know what, Hector,' Jack said. 'You've made a big mistake.'

'If you're going to give me some lecture about how I shouldn't use the virus to –'

Jack raised a hand, cutting him off. 'No,' he said

312

in a level tone. 'That's only one of your weaknesses –
you assume.'

Hector's eyes narrowed. 'Weaknesses?'

Jack glanced around. 'Another mistake is that you
thought, by calling us here at short notice, that I
wouldn't have time to plan anything.'

'You're really bad at bluffing,' Hector said. 'I'm not
going to listen to you, Jack.'

'I didn't have time to plan much,' Jack said.
'But . . . it was enough.'

'Whatever it is you're trying to do, it won't work.' A
self-satisfied smirk spread across Hector's lips
again. 'You haven't got anything. No way out this
time.'

'Your next mistake is . . .' Jack locked his gaze
with Hector's. 'You should never trust your own
eyes.' He glanced at the others. 'Raze.'

Hector frowned at him. 'What did you just say?'

Jack turned to the group. '*Raze*?'

'Oh, sorry.' Raze lowered his bandana and hood.
'All right, mate?' He winked.

Hector's eyes widened. 'Who are you?'

Suddenly, a dark object dropped from above,
behind Hector, Connor, Cloud and Monday.

Slink was hanging upside down from a rope. He

slipped a harness under Noble's arms and around his chest, and the two of them rose silently into the air.

Charlie's rapid winch worked like a charm and it took all of Jack's willpower not to give it away by looking up as they disappeared into the sky above.

He let out a slow breath.

Hector stepped forward and waved a finger at Raze. 'Who is he?'

Jack whistled the Urban Outlaws' code: three musical notes – one short and low, one high, and the last a long mid-tone.

There were three rapid high chirps in reply, which meant Noble was safe.

Hector looked up and scowled. 'What was that?'

'Slink,' Jack said. 'Your next mistake is you should never take your eyes off the only leverage you have.'

Hector spun around. 'Where is he?' He looked at Connor. 'You idiot.'

Connor looked up, but Slink and Noble were nowhere to be seen.

'Hector,' Jack said. '*Focus.*'

Hector turned back, his face twisted in confusion and anger.

Connor pointed at Charlie, Obi, Wren and Raze. 'I'll kill them all right here.'

'No you won't,' Jack said.

Connor slid a hand under his jacket. 'Watch me.'

Jack looked at Cloud. 'Did you check the virus's program?' he asked her.

She nodded.

'No tricks,' Hector said. 'We have it. You can't persuade us otherwise.'

'Yeah,' Jack said. 'You do have the virus.' He kept his focus on Cloud. 'But did you notice the shell?'

Hector glanced at her.

Cloud pulled the laptop and modem from her bag and fired them up. After a moment, she said, 'It's encrypted.'

'What?' Hector said.

'He's put the virus in an encrypted shell.' Cloud stared at Jack. 'He's written a program that surrounds it like a protective cloak.'

'How did you not notice that?' Hector snapped.

Cloud looked at him and hesitated. 'It – it was hidden,' she said. 'I didn't see the file. Now it's activated and sealed the virus.' She glanced at Jack. 'Without the password, it won't run. It's dead.'

Hector's eyes hardened. 'Crack the password.'

Cloud shook her head. 'I can't. Well, not quickly. Without the password, it would take me days just to –'

Hector spun to Jack. 'Give it to me.' He stepped forward, his face inches from Jack's. 'Give me the password.'

Jack refused to be intimidated. 'You're not getting it,' he said, trying to keep his voice level and calm, though his insides were squirming. Not because of Hector's threating behaviour, but because this was the crucial part of his plan.

'Kill one of the others,' Hector said to Connor. He stepped back. 'Let's see if that loosens his tongue.'

'It won't do any good,' Jack said. 'The password is random and linked to personal questions that only I know the answers to. It will be a combination of things, like "What was your mum's maiden name? And your place of birth?" Take the first, second, fourth and seventh letter from the first answer and combine it with the third, fourth and sixth letters from the other.' Jack shrugged. 'I have no way of knowing what the shell program will ask for. There are thirty questions and thousands of combinations of letters.'

Hector looked at Cloud. 'Is he telling the truth?'

She nodded. 'And I can't move the virus back from your server. It's locked down.' She sighed, closed the laptop and stood up. 'We have to go to where it's now stored.'

Hector roared with annoyance.

'I'm not going anywhere with you,' Jack said, keeping his voice casual, 'unless, you release these four.' He pointed at the others.

'No,' Connor said to Hector. 'End it here. *Now.*'

'I want the virus.'

'You're being stupid,' Connor said. 'Don't let some program affect your judgment. Your father made –'

'My father wanted the same thing as I do,' Hector shouted. 'He started all this and I'm going to see it through for him.' Hector's eyes blazed. 'I told you I want the virus. Haven't you been listening to me? Do you have any concept of what I could do with it?' Hector turned slowly to Jack. 'If I let your pathetic friends go, where are my guarantees?'

'You don't have any,' Jack said. 'You just have my word. Release the others and I'll go with you and unlock the virus. Then you can do what you want with me.'

'Jack,' Charlie said. 'You don't have to do this.'

317

'I do.' Jack looked at Hector again. 'It's your call.'

'Don't do it,' Connor warned him.

'Shut up,' Hector snapped. 'I pay you to do what I say. Don't you forget that for one second. When my dad wakes up . . .' He looked at Monday. 'Escort these four out.'

Monday stepped forward. 'Go,' he said in a deep voice, and started shoving Charlie, Obi, Wren and Raze towards the stairs.

Hector stepped up, his face an inch from Jack's. 'If you betray me, I will kill you.'

Jack stared back at him. He didn't doubt Hector's words for a second.

• • •

Fifteen minutes later, Jack, Hector, Cloud and Monday were in the black SUV as Connor drove across Waterloo Bridge.

Jack stared out of the window. The sun was starting to peer above the horizon, bathing the buildings in golden hues.

They turned left after the bridge and then a sharp right. Connor pulled into the alleyway next to a five-star hotel: a popular haunt for film stars and billionaires.

As they climbed out of the SUV, Monday kept a firm grip on Jack's shoulder and they marched to the front of the building.

A doorman, dressed in a top hat and tails, bowed and held the door open.

The hotel foyer had a pale marble floor, red velvet chairs and silk wallpaper, and everything was trimmed in gold. It reminded Jack of a palace.

The concierge behind the reception desk smiled at Hector. 'Good morning, sir.'

Hector strode past him and stood in front of the lift.

After a few seconds, the doors pinged and opened. The bellboy didn't ask Hector for a floor number, he just pressed the button for the eighth floor and the doors slid shut.

They stood in silence as the lift rose. Classical music played quietly.

Connor's eyes burned into Jack.

For the first time, Jack wasn't sure he was going to get out of this mess alive.

The doors opened and Hector marched up the hallway, swiped a card in a lock and walked into a vast hotel suite.

The enormous lounge was furnished with plush

sofas, and there were antiques and fragile-looking ornaments all around.

They escorted Jack through a door to the right and into an office. On the wall, under a brass picture light, hung a dark oil painting. It was of a small wooden boat, crammed with thirteen men, in a storm-tossed sea. The sail was up as the boat crashed over a huge wave.

Jack edged closer.

One of the men actually looked as though he was being sick over the side of the boat.

Monday grabbed Jack's shoulder and spun him around.

Hector opened a cupboard on the far wall, revealing two computer servers. He looked at Cloud and pointed at the right-hand one.

Cloud sat behind the desk and fired up the screen. She typed and clicked for a few seconds, then looked up. 'Ready.'

Monday shoved Jack forward.

Hector stepped in front of him. 'Any more tricks and . . .' He drew a finger across his throat.

Jack had the distinct feeling that tricks or not, Hector's plan was to have him killed anyway.

Cloud stood up and moved out of the way as Jack walked around the desk and sat down.

He looked at the screen. There was a pop-up box, asking for the first, fourth and sixth letter of his biggest phobia, along with the first and third letters of the place he was born.

Jack glanced up at Hector.

'Do it,' Hector said.

Connor pulled back his jacket and gripped his gun.

'Are you sure you want to do this?' Jack asked Hector. 'You can walk away. This is your last chance.'

'No,' Connor said. 'This is *your* last chance.'

Jack didn't take his eyes off Hector.

'I told you to do it,' Hector said.

Jack pulled the keyboard towards him and typed the letters. After a few seconds, the pop-up box disappeared and a new window opened.

Cloud stepped forward, her eyes wide. She pushed Jack out of the way and leant into the screen.

'Is it done?' Hector said. 'Do we have the virus?'

'No.'

'What?'

'Wait.' Cloud typed and clicked.

Hector paced the room, fists balled, his face burning red.

Cloud finally stopped and looked up at him, her eyes full of fear.

'What's he done?' Hector said. 'What's going on?'

'That shell program that was stopping the virus from running.'

'What about it?'

Cloud swallowed. 'The password wasn't to free the virus. It did something else.'

Hector's eyes narrowed. 'What did it do?'

'Opened a port on your network, connected to the internet and sent the program and virus back out.'

'*Out*?' Hector said. 'Out where?'

Cloud shrugged. 'I don't know.'

Hector looked at Jack. 'Where did you send it?'

Jack leant back in the chair and remained tight-lipped.

The computer let out a beep and the screen froze.

Cloud tried a few keys but the keyboard was locked. She shook the mouse and still nothing happened. Slowly, she turned to Jack.

They heard police sirens in the distance.

Jack smiled to himself. The plan was working – the tracker in his shoe had relayed his location, and Charlie and the others had called the cops.

Connor stepped to the window and pulled back

the curtain, as the sirens grew louder. He roared and spun to Jack. 'He's set us up.'

Hector ran around the desk and grabbed Jack by the throat. 'I'm going to keep my promise and kill you.'

'That's not a good idea,' Cloud said.

Hector glanced at her. 'Give me one good reason.'

'Because this is your suite. You live here. If the police find the body of a dead fifteen-year-old kid in this room, they'll arrest all of us.'

Hector's grip tightened. 'I don't care.'

Sirens blared, tyres screeched and car doors slammed.

Connor peered out of the window. 'We're out of time. They're here.'

Cloud turned and strode from the room.

'Where are you going?' Hector called.

'We're getting out of here.'

Hector swore and let go of Jack's throat. As he marched from the room, he said, 'Bring him with us.'

Monday yanked Jack from the chair and they hurried through the suite to the main door.

Cloud was already in the hallway, waiting for them. She pointed at the lift. 'They're on their way up.' She marched to the exit sign at the end of the corridor and burst through into the stairwell.

They hurried down the stairs, with Cloud in the lead, followed by Hector, Connor, Jack and Monday.

At the bottom were two doors. One led to the foyer and the other had a sign on it which read, *PERSONNEL ONLY. KEEP OUT.*

Connor opened the door to the foyer a crack and peered through. He glanced around and pulled back again. 'Five police officers,' he whispered. 'Two by the main door, two by the lifts and the other one is right near us. We go through there and we're –'

'Toast.' Hector looked at Jack and his lip curled. 'If we go down, you're coming with us.'

Jack shrugged. 'Go on then.'

Connor walked over to the door with the sign and peered inside. 'It's a corridor,' he said. 'Come on.'

As they marched along the hallway, Jack glanced up. There was a CCTV camera in the corner. The red LED blinked on and off three times.

Jack smiled to himself and relaxed a little. Obi was back at the Outlaws' bunker and watching what was going on.

At the end of the corridor was another door with a round window.

Connor peered through it. 'Kitchen,' he said. 'There's a door at the other end. That probably leads to the alley where I parked the car.' He glanced back.

Hector gave him the nod. 'Let's go.'

Connor pushed the door open and they strode into the kitchen.

As they walked between stainless-steel kitchen tops, the air was hot and filled with steam. Chefs barked orders at each other and the clatter of cutlery, pans and plates was deafening.

'Hey,' one of the chefs called to the group as they passed. 'Who are you?'

'Never you mind,' Connor said.

Another chef stepped into Connor's path. 'We *do* mind.' He pointed at the door to the stairwell. 'Go back.'

Connor nodded towards the door to the alley. 'We're going through there.'

'No,' the chef said, drawing himself up to his full height. 'You're going back the way you came.'

Connor sighed. He looked at Hector, then at the chef. 'Kitchen, you say?' He opened his jacket, revealing the gun in the holster slung under his arm. 'You sure it's not a shooting range?'

The chef's eyes widened and his gaze moved to a set of knives on the counter next to him.

'I wouldn't advise that,' Connor said, his fingers sliding over the grip of his gun. 'Now, this is your last chance, get out of our way and let us past.'

The door to the stairwell burst open behind them and two police officers stepped into the kitchen, guns drawn.

'Hands above your heads,' one of them shouted.

In one rapid move, Connor spun, pulled his gun out and fired.

The bullet hit the wall, missing one of the cops by a millimetre. Both of them returned fire and bullets ricocheted above Jack's head.

Cloud and Monday drew their own guns and dived behind the counters.

Jack dropped to the floor and lay flat, with his hands over his head.

More shots rang out and people ran past him, shouting. He looked up. One of the cops spoke quickly into a radio, calling for backup.

Jack commando-crawled towards the alleyway door, keeping his head low, as the agents continued to exchange fire with Connor and Cloud.

Someone grabbed Jack's leg.

'Where do you think you're going?' It was Monday. He pulled Jack around the corner and shoved him against a steel cabinet. He peered over the top of the counter, let off two rounds, then ducked as several more shots thudded around him.

Monday sat back and loaded another clip into his gun. He looked at Jack. 'Stay here,' he said, and stepped back around the corner, firing shots.

Suddenly, the lights went out, plunging the kitchen into complete darkness.

There were more shouts and gunshots flashed.

Someone gripped Jack's arm and he tried to pull himself free.

'It's me,' Charlie whispered into his ear. 'I'm wearing night-glasses. I can see.'

Thank God, Jack thought.

'Are you hurt?' she whispered.

'No.' Jack got to his knees. 'Was it you who called the police?'

'Yeah, didn't expect this though.'

Two more flashes started another barrage of gunshots and shouting.

Charlie led Jack around the counter. Each time a gun muzzle flashed, Jack caught a glimpse of the door to the stairwell.

'Wrong way,' Jack whispered.

Charlie stopped. 'No.'

Hurried footsteps passed right in front of them, then when they'd gone, she continued forward. Charlie pushed open the door to the stairwell and slid out of the kitchen.

A red light glowed above the door to the foyer and they stood, catching their breaths. Charlie went to grab the handle when the door opened and three more cops rushed in. They shone their torches on Jack and Charlie.

'Get out of here, kids,' the lead one said, drawing his gun. 'Hurry, and don't look back.'

'Thank you,' Charlie said in a mock shaky voice. She took Jack's hand and pushed through the door to the foyer.

Several more police officers and a SWAT team were getting ready to go in.

A cop saw Jack and Charlie. He ran over to them and ushered them across the foyer and out of the building.

Outside, the street was filled with flashing blue lights and the sky was a blood red.

The cop pointed past a cordoned-off area. 'Go. That way.'

Other cops waved Jack and Charlie on as they jogged down the road. They ducked under the police tape and vanished into the crowd.

They heard the distinct sound of more gun-shots.

Slink and Wren appeared by their sides.

'Are you two OK?' Jack asked.

'Course,' Slink said. 'You all right?'

'Yeah,' Jack replied. 'Thanks for getting the lights.' Without the convenient blackout, Jack would've still been in there. Probably shot. Possibly dead.

'It wasn't me this time,' Slink said, pointing at Wren. 'She was the only one who could squeeze through the air vent.'

Wren puffed her chest out.

'Thanks,' Jack said. 'You guys saved my life.' He looked at the alleyway next to the hotel. 'Their car,' he said in sudden realisation. 'We should disable it. Stop them from escaping.' He took a step forward, but Charlie grabbed his arm.

She put a finger to her ear. 'Obi says Hector, Connor and Cloud have already made it to the car.' She paused. 'They're driving off. We're too late.'

Jack swore.

Several police radios squawked and cops ran to their cars, jumped in and gave chase, sirens blaring.

'Come on,' Jack said, pulling up his hood. 'Time to get out of here.'

CHAPTER FIFTEEN

A WEEK LATER, JACK AND CHARLIE WERE SITTING on a bench in Covent Garden. It was a bright, cloud-free day and people bustled past, without a second glance. On the bench between them, partly obscured by her bag, Charlie held the directional microphone. They slipped earphones in and she pointed it at a café opposite.

Obi was sitting at a metal table outside and he had just ordered a huge chocolate brownie. He'd insisted that Jack and Charlie come with him and listen to the conversation.

A woman in her early-to-mid twenties walked up. She had a slim figure, light brown hair and wore a fast-food restaurant uniform.

Jack knew this had to be Jessica – Obi's sister.

Obi swallowed and wiped chocolate from his mouth. 'Hi. How are you?' he said.

Jessica dropped into the chair opposite. 'I'm all right.' She glanced at the remains of the brownie. 'You've got to stop eating rubbish.'

'Yeah.' Obi half smiled. 'You know I'm sorry, right?'

Jessica frowned. 'Sorry for what?'

Obi picked up a napkin and twisted it in his hands. 'It's my fault you had an argument with our uncle.'

'Where did that come from?' Jessica said. 'We've been through this before – it was *not* your fault. You can't blame yourself.'

Obi continued to twist the napkin around his fingers.

Jessica leant over the table and took it from him. 'Why do you even think that?'

Obi took a deep breath and looked at her. 'You were arguing about me. You had a go at him.'

'He was treating you badly,' Jessica said.

'Yeah,' Obi said. 'But –' He shrugged.

Neither of them spoke for a moment.

Finally, Jessica said, 'Look, I never blamed you for him chucking me out of the house. I was old enough to look after myself.' She traced her fingers along the pattern in the table. 'When I realised he'd sent you to that home, I tried to get him to take you back, you know that, but he wouldn't. I just wish I'd had the money to look after you myself.'

'I'm doing OK,' Obi said.

'Are you ever going to tell me where you live?'

'You wouldn't believe me.'

Jessica looked away, seeming to wrestle with her own conscience.

'It's not that I don't want to tell you,' Obi said. 'I just – I don't – I didn't want to –'

Jessica looked back at him. 'Are you in trouble?'

Obi shook his head.

'Are you safe?'

Obi nodded.

'Please tell me where you're staying.'

'I live with my friends.'

'Who are they?' Jessica's eyes hardened. 'What are you up to?'

'Nothing bad,' Obi said. 'We help people.'

Jessica frowned at this.

'Trust me, Jess. I will tell you one day, I promise.'

Jessica sighed and said, 'So, what's new with you?'

'I have something.' Obi reached into the backpack by his chair and pulled out the Manila envelope. He looked at it, then slid it across the table.

Jessica stared. 'What's this?'

'Your future,' Obi said. He took a breath. '*Our* future.'

Jessica folded her arms again.

'Take a look,' Obi said. 'Please?'

She picked up the envelope. Jessica frowned at the handwriting on the front, then slid out the paper, unfolded it and started to read.

Obi stared intently at her.

As the seconds turned into minutes, Jessica's eyes widened and her mouth opened in shock. Finally, when she had finished reading, she held the paper in her shaking hands and looked at Obi again. 'This –' Her voice cracked and she swallowed. 'This is real?' she said in a whisper.

Obi nodded. 'Yep.'

She leant forward. 'How – how did you get this?'

'From the mansion in France.'

Jessica's eyebrows lifted. 'You went to France?'

Obi nodded again. 'My friends helped me.'

Jessica's eyes glazed over and she stared unseeing into the distance.

'Jess,' Obi said. 'You know what this means? You don't have to work in that place any more. You can run the company. Mum and Dad's business. It's ours.'

Jessica's eyes focused on him. 'I don't know how to run a company.'

'Yeah, you do,' Obi said. 'Dad always said you'd –' He stopped himself.

They stared at each other.

Finally, Jessica seemed to regain her senses. 'What about you? We can be a family again. You can come home.'

'I will one day,' Obi said. 'But not just yet.'

'Why not?'

'I'm not ready.'

'But,' Jessica said, 'the money. You're entitled to half.'

'Hold on to it and I'll let you know if I need any.'

Jessica's eyebrows rose at that. 'Are you sure?'

Obi nodded and grinned.

Jessica reached across the table and squeezed his hand. After a moment, she let go and stood up. She held up the will. 'I'll take this to a solicitor.' And started to walk away.

Obi called after her, 'Hey, Jess.'

She turned back. 'Yeah?'

'You'll be great, I know it.'

Jess smiled. 'Are we seeing each other again next week?'

'*Sure*,' Obi said. 'You can buy the brownies.'

'Fine,' Jessica said. 'And you're sure you're all right?'

Obi nodded. 'Never better.'

Jessica hesitated for a moment, then turned and walked away.

Jack looked back at Obi and could've sworn he saw a glimmer of a tear.

'Right,' Charlie said, slipping the directional microphone into her bag and zipping it up. 'Now that all the excitement's over, back to the real world.' She looked at Jack. 'We're out of supplies, so who's going to do the shopping?'

Jack groaned. 'Flip you for it?' He pulled a coin from his pocket. 'Heads you go, tails I go.'

Charlie's eyes narrowed. 'OK.'

Jack tossed the coin into the air but before he'd caught it again Charlie snatched it from him.

She examined the coin and swore. 'You idiot.' She held it up. The coin was double-headed. 'You tricked me.' Her eyes went wide as she remembered the other times Jack had used it.

'Hey, guys,' Obi said. 'Fancy a takeaway?'

Charlie stood up. 'Sure, why not?'

Jack got to his feet and pulled the USB drive from his pocket.

'What's that?' Charlie asked him.

'The virus. I wasn't comfortable keeping it on the

bunker's servers, just in case it did more damage and escaped again.'

'What are you going to do with it?' Obi said.

Jack gazed at the USB drive for a moment. He sighed, the power was tempting but – he dropped it to the ground.

'Jack,' Charlie said. 'No –'

But it was too late – he stamped on the USB stick, breaking it into pieces.

Charlie and Obi stared open-mouthed.

'What did you just do?' Charlie breathed.

'Solved a problem.'

She looked at him. 'What problem?'

'I know that, as long as the virus existed, I'd be tempted to use it.' Jack half smiled and walked away.

Charlie and Obi followed him in stunned silence.

• • •

When Jack, Charlie and Obi got back to the bunker, Slink and Wren were practically bouncing off the walls with excitement.

'What's going on?' Charlie said, setting down three pizza boxes.

'You're not going to believe this,' Slink said. He

hurried over to Obi's chair and spun the main monitor to face them.

Jack, Charlie and Obi walked towards it.

Jack frowned. 'What's this?'

'A signal from your program popped up on the screen. You know, the one you used to trap the virus? Well, it opened a direct line to the bunker and went to transmit itself, but stopped.'

Jack glanced at Obi. 'That's impossible. I destroyed it. Unless –' Jack's blood ran cold and he felt the colour drain from his face.

'Unless what?' Charlie said.

'The other server in his apartment,' Jack said under his breath. 'Oh, my God.' Now it made sense. *Too little, too late.*

'What are you on about?' Slink said.

Jack turned to them. 'Hector. He had another server in his apartment. I didn't think anything of it at the time.' Jack closed his eyes. 'Now I under-stand.'

'Understand what?' Slink said.

'Hector's cloned the virus. He's copied it.'

'Wait,' Charlie said. 'I thought you said that's impossible.'

'It is.' Jack opened his eyes again. 'It was. But I

338

gave Hector another way to do it. It's my fault.' He looked at them. 'Don't you see? I wrapped the virus in my own program, right? Hector's copied the entire thing. And now, Cloud has had the time she needed to hack into my program.' He looked at the screen. 'Where did the signal come from?'

Obi climbed into his chair. 'Looks like they've severed the connection now.'

'They would,' Charlie said. 'Can't risk the virus escaping to the internet again.'

'I think I can still find a location,' Obi said. 'I'll check the logs.'

'Let me get this straight,' Charlie said. 'Hector has managed to copy the virus?'

Jack nodded slowly. 'We need to stop Hector before he figures out how the virus works and uses it to hack every secure system in the world.'

Obi brought up a map. 'The signal came from here.'

Jack stared at a pulsating red dot over America. 'New York.' He turned to Charlie. 'We have to make a call.'

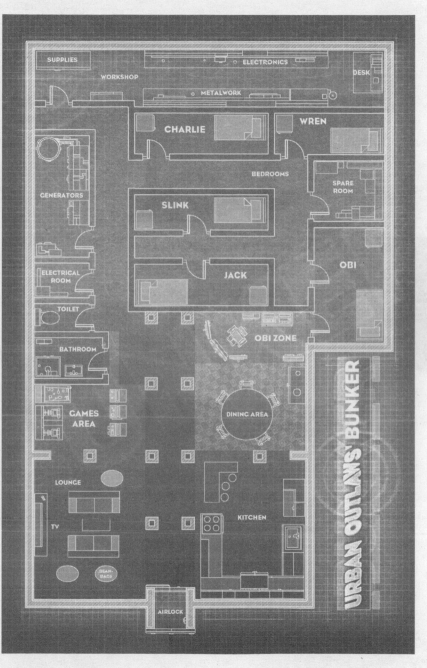

THE URBAN

JACK

HACKER NAME: **ACHILLES**
REAL NAME: **JACK FENTON**
AGE: **15**
SPECIAL SKILL: **HACKING**
LIKES: **PHYSICS**
DISLIKES: **DUBSTEP**
GREATEST FEAR: **HEIGHTS**

CHARLIE

HACKER NAME: **PANDORA**
REAL NAME: **CHARLOTTE CAINE**
AGE: **15**
SPECIAL SKILL: **MAKING GADGETS**
LIKES: **COMPUTER GAMES**
DISLIKES: **GROSS HABITS**
GREATEST FEAR: **FIRE**

OUTLAWS

OBI

URBAN OUTLAWS

HACKER NAME: **OBI**
REAL NAME: **JOSEPH HARLINGTON**
AGE: **14**
SPECIAL SKILL: **SURVEILLANCE**
LIKES: **CONSPIRACY THEORIES**
DISLIKES: **SALAD!**
GREATEST FEAR:
ANYTHING THAT CRAWLS

SLINK

HACKER NAME: **SLINK**
REAL NAME: **TOM SMITH**
AGE: **12**
SPECIAL SKILL: **FREE RUNNING**
LIKES: **ART!**
DISLIKES: **QUIET DUBSTEP**
GREATEST FEAR: **NOTHING**

WREN

HACKER NAME: **WREN**
REAL NAME: **JENNIFER JENKINS**
AGE: **10**
SPECIAL SKILL: **DECOY/PICKPOCKET**
LIKES: **CARTOONS**
DISLIKES: **HOSPITALS**
GREATEST FEAR: **DROWNING**

PETER JAY BLACK loves gadgets, films and things that make him laugh so hard he thinks he might pass out. He went to Arts University Bournemouth and a career in IT followed. One day, a team of super-skilled kids popped into his head and, writing in a Hollywood apartment, he brought them to life. Peter lives in Dorset and in his spare time he enjoys collecting unusual artefacts like Neolithic arrowheads, ancient Egyptian rings and fossilised dinosaur poo.

WIN AN XBOX ONE!

For a chance to get your hands on this amazing prize, simply tell us what your RANDOM ACT OF KINDNESS would be.

Email your answer to childrensmarketing@bloomsbury.com with **#UrbanRAKing** in the subject line.

OR

Share it across social media using **#UrbanRAKing** and tagging @kidsbloomsbury.

For more information on how to enter, closing dates and terms and conditions, visit **urbanoutlawsbunker.com/competition**.